the fox was ever the hunter

a novel

Herta Müller

Translated by Philip Boehm

Portobello

First published in Great Britain by Portobello Books in 2016
This paperback edition published by Portobello Books in 2017

Portobello Books
12 Addison Avenue
London
W11 4QR

First published in the United States in 2016 by Metropolitan Books,
Henry Holt and Company, LLC, New York.

Originally published in Germany in 1992 under the title
Der Fuchs war damals schon der Jäger by Rowohlt Verlag.

The translator would like to thank the John Simon Guggenheim
Memorial Foundation and the Rockefeller Foundation Bellagio Center
for their generous support in making this book available in English.

A CIP catalogue record for this book
is available from the British Library.

1 3 5 7 9 10 8 6 4 2

ISBN 978 1 84627 477 0 (paperback)
ISBN 978 1 84627 478 7 (ebook)

Designed by Kelly S. Too

Offset by M Rules

Printed and bound by
CPI Group (UK) Ltd, Croydon, CR0 4YY

www.portobellobooks.com

That doesn't matter, I said to myself.
Doesn't matter at all.

—*Venedikt Yerofeyev*

CONTENTS

THE FOX WAS EVER THE HUNTER

The way of the apple worm

The ant is carrying a dead fly three times its size. The ant can't see the way ahead, it flips the fly around and crawls back. Adina doesn't want to block the ant's path so she pulls in her elbow. A clump of tar next to her knee glistens as it seethes in the sun. Adina dabs at the tar with her finger, raising a thin thread that stiffens in the air before it snaps.

The ant has the head of a pin, the sun can't find any place to burn. The sun stings. The ant loses its way. It crawls but is not alive, the human eye does not consider it an animal. The spike heads of the grasses on the outskirts of town crawl the same way. The fly is alive because it's three times the size of the ant and because it's being carried, the human eye does consider the fly an animal.

Clara is blinded by the blazing pumpkin of the sun and doesn't see the fly. She sits with her legs apart and rests her hands between her knees. Pubic hair shows where her swimsuit cuts into her thighs. Below her pubic hair is a pair of scissors, a spool of white thread, sunglasses and a thimble. Clara is sewing a summer blouse for herself. The needle dives, the thread advances, the needle pricks her finger and Clara licks the blood and spits out a shorthand curse involving ice and thread: your mother on the ice. A curse implying unspeakable things done to the mother of the needle. When Clara curses, everything has a mother.

The mother of the needle is the place that bleeds. The mother of the needle is the oldest needle in the world, the one that gave birth to all needles. The mother of the needle watches out for all her children, she is always looking for a finger to stab on every sewing hand in the world. The world contained in the curse is tiny, tucked under a cluster of needles and a clot of blood. And the mother of all thread is there too, lurking inside the curse, a massive tangle looming over the world.

All this heat and you're going on about ice, says Adina, as Clara's jawbones grind away while her tongue beats inside her mouth. Whenever she curses, Clara's face wrinkles up, because every word is a well-aimed bullet fired from her lips and every word hits its mark. As well as the mother of its mark.

Clara lies down on the blanket next to Adina. Adina is naked, Clara is wearing her swimsuit bottom and nothing else.

Curses are cold. They have no need of dahlias or bread or apples or summer. Curses are not for smelling and not for eating. Only for churning up and laying down flat, for an instant of rage and a long time keeping still. Curses lower the throbbing of the temples into the wrist and hoist the dull heartbeat into the ear. Curses swell and choke on themselves.

Once a curse is lifted, it never existed.

The blanket is spread out on the roof of the apartment block, which is surrounded by poplars. The poplars rise higher than all the city roofs and are draped with green, they don't show individual leaves, only a wash of foliage. They don't swish, they whoosh. The foliage rises straight up on the poplars just like the branches, the wood cannot be seen. And where nothing else can reach, the poplars carve the hot air. The poplars are green knives.

When Adina stares at the poplars too long, they dig their knives inside her throat and twist them from side to side. Then her throat gets dizzy. And her forehead senses that no afternoon is capable of holding even a single poplar for the time the light takes to sink behind the factory into the evening. The evening ought to hurry, the night might succeed in holding the poplars, because then they can't be seen.

The day is shattered by the beating of rugs between apartment blocks, the blows echo up to the roof and collapse one onto the other, the way Clara's words do when she curses.

The beating of rugs cannot hoist the dull heartbeat into the ear.

Clara is tired after her curse, and the sky is so empty she closes her eyes, which are blinded by the light, while Adina opens her eyes wide and gazes far too long into the emptiness. From high overhead, beyond the reach even of the green knives, a taut thread of hot air stretches straight down to her eyes. And from this thread hangs the weight of the city.

That morning at school a child said to Adina, the sky looks so different today. A boy who's always very still when he's with the others. His eyes are set far apart, which makes his temples look narrow. My mother woke me up at four o'clock this morning, he said, and she gave me the key because she had to go to the train station. I walked out to the gate with her. When we were going through the courtyard the sky was so close I could feel it on my shoulder. I could have leaned back against it, but I didn't want to scare my mother. When I went back by myself I could see right through all the stones. So I hurried as fast as I could. The door to our building looked different, the wood was empty. I could have slept another three hours, the child said, but I never fell back asleep. And even though I wasn't sleeping I still woke up scared. Only maybe I really did sleep, because my eyes felt all pinched up. I had this dream that I was lying in the sun next to the water and I had this blister on my stomach. I pulled the skin off the blister but it didn't hurt. Because under my skin was stone. Then the wind blew and lifted the water into the air, but it wasn't water at all, just a wrinkled cloth. And there weren't any stones underneath either, only flesh.

The boy laughed into that last sentence, and into the silence that followed. His teeth were like gravel, the blackened half teeth and the smooth white ones. The age in his face couldn't stand his childish voice. The boy's face smelled like stale fruit.

It was the smell of old women who put on so much powder it starts to wilt just like their skin. Women whose hands quiver in front of the mirror, who smudge lipstick on their teeth and then a little while later inspect their fingers against the mirror. Whose nails are buffed and ringed with white.

When the boy stood in the school yard together with the other children, the blotch on his cheek was the clamp of loneliness.

And the spot grew, because slanting light was falling over the poplars.

Clara has dozed off in the sun, her sleep carries her far away and leaves Adina alone. The beating of rugs shatters the summer into shells of green. And the whoosh of the poplars contains the green shells of all the summers left behind. All the years when you're still a child and growing and nevertheless sense that each single day goes tumbling off some cliff whenever evening comes. Days of childhood, with square-cut hair and dried mud in the outskirts of town, dust behind the streetcar, and on the sidewalk the footsteps of tall, emaciated men earning money to buy bread.

The outskirts were attached to the town with wires and pipes and a bridge that had no river. The outskirts were open at both ends, just like the walls, the roads and the lines of trees. The city streetcars went whooshing into the town at one of the ends, where the factories blew smoke into the sky above the bridge that had no river. At times the whooshing and the smoke were all the same thing. At the other end, farmland gnawed away at the outskirts, and the fields of leafy beets stretched far into the countryside. Farther away still was a village, the white walls gleaming in the distance looked no bigger than a hand. Suspended between the village and the bridge that had no river were sheep. The sheep didn't eat the beet leaves, only the grass that grew along the way, before the summer was out they had devoured the entire lane. Then they gathered at the edge of town and licked the walls of the factory.

The factory was large, with buildings on both sides of the

bridge without water. From behind the walls came the screaming of cows and pigs. At night their horns and hooves were burned, the acrid stench wafted into the outskirts. The factory was a slaughterhouse.

In the morning, while it was still dark, roosters crowed. They walked through the gray inner courtyards the same way the emaciated men walked on the street. And they had the same look.

The men rode the streetcar to the last stop and then crossed the bridge. On the bridge the sky hung low, and when it was red, the men had red cockscombs in their hair. The local barber told Adina's father that there was nothing more beautiful than a cockscomb for the heroes of labor.

Adina had asked the barber about the red combs because he knew every scalp and every whorl. He said whorls are for hair what wings are for roosters. So even though no one could say exactly when, Adina knew that each of the emaciated men would at some point go flying over the bridge.

Because sometimes the roosters did go flying over the fences. Before taking off they would drink water out of empty food cans in the courtyards. At night the roosters slept in shoe boxes. When the trees turned cold at night, cats crawled into the boxes as well.

It was exactly seventy steps from the last stop to the bridge that had no river—Adina had counted them. The last stop on one side of the street was the first on the other. At the last stop the men climbed out slowly, and at the first the women climbed in quickly. Early in the morning they ran to catch the streetcar with matted hair and flying purses and sweat stains under their arms. The stains were often dried out and rimmed with white. Their nail polish was eaten away by machine oil and rust. And even as they rushed to catch the streetcar their faces already carried the weariness from the wire factory.

At the sound of the first streetcars Adina woke up. She felt cold in her summer dress. The dress had a pattern of trees, but the tops were upside down. The seamstress had stitched the material the wrong way.

The seamstress lived in two small rooms, the floor was full of angles and the walls had bellied out from the damp. The windows opened onto the courtyard. One window had a sign propped up that said COOPERATIVE OF PROGRESS.

The seamstress called the rooms the WORKSHOP. Every surface—table, bed, chairs, chest and even the floor—was covered with snippets and scraps. And each piece of fabric had a piece of paper with a name. A wooden crate behind the bed held a sack full of scraps. On the crate was a label NO LONGER OF USE.

The seamstress kept her clients' measurements in a small notebook. Anyone who'd been coming for years was considered a longtimer. Whoever came rarely, by chance, or only once was a short-termer. If a longtimer brought some material, the seamstress didn't need to take more measurements, except for one woman who went into the slaughterhouse every day and was as emaciated as the men—for her the seamstress had to take new measurements every time. She held the tape in her mouth and said, really, you'd be better off going to the vet and having him outfit you with a dress instead of me. Every summer you get thinner and thinner. Pretty soon my notebook will get filled up with just your bones.

Several times a year the woman brought the seamstress a new notebook. On the cover it said BRIGADE NOTEBOOK and above the columns on each page it said LIVE WEIGHT and SLAUGHTER WEIGHT.

Adina was never allowed to go barefoot in the workshop, the scraps and snippets littering the floor were full of pins. Only the seamstress knew how to move without getting pricked. Once a week she crawled through the rooms with a magnet and all the pins and needles jumped into her hand.

When Adina tried on the dress, her mother said to the seamstress, can't you see that the trees are growing the wrong way, you turned the fabric upside down. The seamstress could still have turned it right side up, the fabric was only basted with white thread. But with two pins in her mouth she said, what's important is front and back, and that the zipper's on the left. Besides, when I look from here, the bottom is the top. She lowered her face to the floor. That's how the chickens see it, she said. And the dwarves, said Adina. Her mother looked out the window at the courtyard.

On the side of the courtyard that faced the street was a display window with crosses, stovepipes and watering cans made of tin. They were propped up with old newspapers, and in front of the display was an embroidered blanket with a tin sign on top that said COOPERATIVE OF PROGRESS.

The crosses, stovepipes and watering cans shuddered whenever the streetcar passed by. But they didn't tip over.

Behind the display window was a table with scissors, pliers and screws, behind the table sat a man. He was a tinsmith. He wore a leather apron. His wedding ring hung on a string around his neck, because both hands were missing the ring finger.

Some people said that his first wife had been dead a long time, and that he never found a second because he kept his wedding ring around his neck. The barber claimed that the tinsmith had never had a wife at all, that he'd used the same ring four times to get engaged but never married. If there were enough crosses, stovepipes and watering cans to fill the display window, he could turn to repairing old pots and pans.

When the streetcar passed, the faces in the tram hovered in the display window between the stovepipes and crosses. On the watering cans the faces were wavy from the movement and from the sheen of the tin. Once the streetcar moved on, the only thing left on the watering cans was the gleam of trampled snow.

For several summers Adina wore her dress with the falling trees. Every summer Adina grew taller, and the dress got shorter. And every summer the trees hung upside down and they felt as heavy as ever. Underneath the rising trees that lined the sidewalk, the girl from the outskirts of town had a shy face. The shade never covered it entirely. Her shaded cheek stayed cool, and Adina had the feeling she could zip it open or shut, like her dress. Her cheek in the sunlight turned hot and soft.

After a summer rain that failed to cool off the paving stones, black chains of ants crawled inside the cracks in the courtyard. Adina took a tube from a circular knitting needle and poured sugar water into the transparent plastic and set the tube in one of the cracks. The ants crawled inside and lined up: head, abdomen, head, abdomen. Adina lit a match, sealed the ends of the tube and hung it around her neck. Stepping to the mirror she saw that the necklace was alive, even though the ants were dead, stuck to the sugar, each in the place where it had suffocated.

Only when the ants were in the tube did the human eye consider them animals.

Adina went to the barber every week, because her hair grew

quickly and she wasn't allowed to let it cover her ears. On the way she passed the display window with the crosses, stovepipes and watering cans. The tinsmith waved and she went inside. He handed her a cone rolled from newspaper. The cone had cherries in May, apricots as early as June, and grapes just a little later, even though no ripe ones could be found in any of the gardens. At the time Adina was convinced that the newspaper caused the change of fruit.

When he handed her the cone the tinsmith said eat the fruit now or else it'll go bad. And she started to eat very quickly, fearing it might go bad even while he was talking. Then the tinsmith said, eat slowly so you can savor every bite for a long time.

She chewed and swallowed and watched as the flame flickered from the soldering iron, covering and filling the pits in the bottom of the pot. The filled holes gleamed like the stovepipes, watering cans and crosses in the window. When fire stops chewing your pot, death will bite you in the ass, said the tinsmith.

One afternoon Adina went to get her haircut wearing her necklace of ants. She sat in front of the big mirror and let her legs dangle off the chair. The barber combed down her hair and when he reached her neck he stopped, shielded his eyes with the comb, and said, that's it, either the ants go this minute or else you do.

A man was sleeping in the corner. The barber's cat was sprawled across his thighs, also sleeping. The man was emaciated and had a cockscomb every morning when he crossed the bridge on his way to the slaughterhouse. He woke with a start and flung the cat out the door. I've got enough dead animals in the slaughterhouse, he shouted, then spat on the floor.

The floor was matted with hair clippings from emaciated men who all knew one another. The hair was brittle, dark gray, light gray and white and made the floor seem like a giant scalp. Cockroaches crawled among the strands. The hair moved up and down. The hair was alive because it was being carried by the cockroaches. But it was not alive on the heads of the men.

The barber dropped his scissors into the open drawer, I can't cut your hair like this, he said, I can feel the ants crawling inside my clothes. He jerked his shirt out of his pants and scratched himself. His fingers left red marks on his stomach. Mother of ants, he cursed. Mother of corpses, said the man from the slaughterhouse. Suddenly the mirror moved and Adina saw herself cut off by the drawer, her feet looked like they were hanging from a roof. She ran out the door and past the cat, who gazed after her with more than its own two eyes.

A week later the barber gave Adina some sweets. The candy had hair sticking to it that scratched her tongue. Adina tried to spit out the hair, but the barber told her it was good for cleaning the throat.

The candy scratched inside her mouth and Adina asked when the man who had flung the cat outside was going to die. The barber crammed a handful of candy into his mouth and said, when a man's had enough hair cut to fill a stamped-down sack, and the sack weighs the same as the man, the man dies. I put all the men's hair into a sack and stamp it down and wait until it's full, said the barber. I don't weigh the hair on the scale, I weigh it with my eyes. I know how much hair I've cut off every one of my customers over the years. My eyes can feel the weight. And I'm never mistaken. He blew on the back of Adina's neck.

The client who threw out the cat will come here seven or eight more times, he said. That's why I didn't say anything, even though the cat hasn't eaten a thing since. I don't want to send a longtime client into the unknown with some other barber for his last haircuts. A wrinkle curled up from his mouth and sliced into his cheek.

Clara sits up on the blanket to put on her summer blouse. The thimble on her forefinger burns in the sun. Her legs are bony, in one motion she pulls them close to her chest and rocks forward as she puts on the blouse. It's the movement of a bony bird who doesn't need to do anything except gaze into the summer and be beautiful. The nearby poplar knife watches. The stubble growing back inside her shaved armpits has already turned into the chin of the man she's talking about. A man with style, she says, is someone I've never met. But I wish.

Clara laughs and straightens out her legs. Her wish is stoked by the sun and dizzied by the roof. Her head knows nothing of the green knives of the poplars, the edge of the roof, the clouds, the city. And that this roof in the sun is full of ants carrying dead flies. And that this roof in the sun is nothing more than a cliff in the sky.

The summer dress with the falling trees and the zipper made Adina forever wary of clothes. She often went to the seamstress's workshop, where she would measure the lives of the women by the weight of the fabric scraps. She would sit and watch, determined to size up each client. She knew which woman's scraps would soon fill a stamped-down sack that weighed as much as the woman. And she knew that after four more dresses, the woman from the slaughterhouse would die.

Clara takes a small, red-flecked summer apple out of her bag and holds it under Adina's chin. The thimble glows, its sharp edge barely missing the apple skin. A small apple with a long, woody stem that takes up too much of what should have been flesh. Adina takes a deep bite. Spit it out, says Clara, there's a worm. The fruit is burrowed with a brown, crumbly thread. Adina swallows what she's bitten off, worm and all. It's just an apple worm, she says, it grows inside the apple, it's made of apple flesh. It doesn't grow inside the apple, says Clara, it crawls inside, eats its way through and then crawls back out. That is its way.

Adina eats, the bite crunches in her ear, what's it supposed to do outside, she says, it's nothing but apple, it's white and eats white flesh and shits a brown path, once it eats its way through the apple it dies. That is its way.

Clara's eyes are small and without any makeup. The sky is empty and the poplar knives stand upright and green. Clara says nothing, she lies down on the blanket, her pupils roll down straight toward her mouth and her eyes close.

A cloud hangs over the apartment block, white and churning. Old folk who die in summer float for a while above the city, lingering between bed and grave.

Clara and the summer old folk are lying in the same sleep. Adina feels the way of the apple worm in her stomach. It runs through her pubic hair down the inside of her thighs and into the hollows of her knees.

The man inside his own hand

A shadow follows a woman, the woman is small and crooked, the shadow keeps its distance. The woman walks across the grass and sits on a bench outside the apartment block.

The woman sits, the shadow stops. The shadow doesn't belong to the woman, just as the shadow of the wall doesn't belong to the wall. The shadows have abandoned the things they belong to. They belong only to the late afternoon, which is now past.

Dahlias have been planted below the lowest row of windows in the apartment block. The flowers are wide open, the hot air has turned their edges to paper. The dahlias peer into kitchens and into rooms, into bowls and into beds.

Smoke reeking of burned onions flies out of one of the kitchen windows and onto the street. A tapestry over the oven inside shows a stag in a forest glade. The stag is the same brown as the colander on the table. A woman licks a wooden spoon, a child stands on a chair, crying. The child has a bib around his neck. The woman uses it to wipe the tears from his face.

The child is too big to be standing on the chair, too big to be wearing a bib. The woman has a blue mark on her elbow. A man's voice shouts, those onions stink and you look like a cow bending over the pot like that, I'm getting the hell out of here, and as far as I can go, too. The woman looks inside the pot, blows into the smoke. In a quiet, stern voice she says, go ahead, pack your shitty things in a suitcase and crawl right back inside your mother. The man jerks the woman by the hair and slaps her in the face. Then the woman stands crying next to the child, while the boy quietly stares at the window.

You were on the roof, says the child, and I saw your butt. The man spits out the window right past the dahlias. He's naked from the waist up, his chest has several blue marks. What's there to see, he says, watch and I'll spit right between your eyes. His spit lands on the sidewalk, together with the shell of a sunflower seed. There's a lot more to see looking out of my ass than at it, says the man. The child laughs, the woman lifts the child from the chair and holds him close. You're laughing, you're growing, she says, you're getting bigger and bigger, and he's going to beat me to death. The man laughs quietly, then loudly. You took him up on the roof didn't you, says the woman.

Every step of the sidewalk is spattered with spit and sprinkled with cigarette butts and sunflower seed husks. And now and then a squashed dahlia. On the curb is a page torn from a school notebook with the sentence, the speed of the blue tractor is six times greater than the speed of the red tractor.

School-day handwriting, the letters in one word falling on their back and in another on their face. And warts on the children's fingers, dirt on the warts, clusters of warts like gray berries, fingers like turkey necks.

Warts can also spread through contact with objects, said Paul, they can migrate onto any skin. Every day Adina touches the children's notebooks and hands. The chalk scrapes against the blackboard, every word she writes could turn into a wart. The eyes in the faces are tired, they are not listening. Then the bell rings, and Adina goes to the teachers' bathroom and looks in the mirror. She studies her face and neck, searching for a wart. The chalk eats away at her fingers.

The wart clusters on the children are full of all the grabbing, all the pushing and kicking, squeezing and shoving, and full of all the bullying and bruising. They contain eager crushes and cruel snubs, the cunning calculation of mothers and fathers, relatives and neighbors and strangers. And if eyes well up or a tooth breaks or an ear bleeds there is simply a shrug of the shoulders.

A trolleybus passes by, windows lit, two sections connected by a wrinkled rubber-coated sleeve, an accordion. The horns glide along the wire overhead, the accordion opens and closes, dust billows from the bellows. The dust is gray, with fine hairs, and is warmer than the evening air. If the trolley is moving the city has electricity. The horns spray sparks into the trees, leaves drop onto the sidewalk from branches that lie too low. The poplars tower over all the streets, in the twilight they are darker than other trees.

A man walks in front of Adina, carrying a flashlight. The city is often without power, flashlights are an extension of the hand. On pitch-black streets the night is all of one piece, and a person on foot is nothing but a sound. The man holds his flashlight with the bulb pointed backward. Evening pulls the last white thread through the end of the street. White tureens and stainless spoons shimmer in the display window. The man has yet to turn his flashlight on, he's waiting until the end of one little street falls into the next. The minute he turns on the flashlight, he disappears. He becomes a man inside his own hand.

The electricity isn't switched off until it's completely dark. Then the shoe factory no longer hums, and a candle burns at the gatehouse, where a man's sleeve can be seen beside the candle. In front of the gatehouse is a dog that's completely invisible except for a pair of glowing eyes. But his bark can be heard, and his paws on the asphalt.

The poplars advance onto every street. The houses crowd together. Candles are lit behind curtains. Parents hold their children up to the light because they want to look at their cheeks one more time before the next morning.

Where the shrubbery is dense, night lurks poised between the foliage and assault. If the city is without power and dark, the night comes from below. First it cuts off the legs. The shoulders are still draped with a gray light, just enough for shaking heads or shutting eyes. But not enough to see by.

Only occasionally do the puddles glow, but not for long, because the ground is thirsty and the summer is dry, after weeks and weeks of dust. A shrub grazes Adina's shoulder. It has restless white flowers with a heavy, insistent fragrance. Adina switches on her flashlight, a circle falls into the dark, an egg. Inside the circle is a head with a beak. The light is not enough to see by, merely enough to make sure the night can't devour all of Adina's back, only half.

The roses outside the apartment block weave a covering full of holes, a colander of dirty leaves and dirty stars. The night pushes the roses out of the city.

The forelock

The newspaper feels rough to the touch, but the dictator's forelock stands out smooth and glossy, slick and shiny with pomade. The big flattened curl pushes all the smaller curls to the back of the head, where they get swallowed by the paper. On the rough newsprint are the words: The beloved son of the people.

Everything that shines also sees.

The forelock shines. It peers into the country every day, and it sees. Every day the dictator's framed image takes up half the table. And the face below the curl takes up both hands when Adina rests them side by side. She looks straight into the void, and swallows her own breath.

The black inside the dictator's eye mirrors the shape and size of Adina's thumbnails, if she crooks her thumbs just slightly. The black inside the eye stares out of the newspaper every day, peering into the country.

The optic nerve runs deep into the land. Towns and villages are squeezed together in one place, torn apart in another. Roads lose themselves in the fields, stopping at graves or by bridges or in front of trees. And trees strangle one another where they were never planted. Dogs stray, and where there are no houses they have long forgotten how to bark. They lose their winter coats, then their summer coats, they're alternately shy and then savage when least expected. They are afraid and their paws smack their foreheads while they run, before they bite.

And wherever the light from the black inside the eye falls, people feel the place where they are standing, the ground beneath their feet, they feel it rising steeply up their throat and sloping sharply down their back.

The light from the black inside the eye falls on the café, too, and on the park, and on the iron tables and chairs that are wrought into leaves and stems, as thin and white as twine. Except they're heavier than they seem when a person tries to lift or slide them, because eyes are focused on the water and fingers are not expecting iron.

The path next to the café runs along the river, the river runs along the path. Fishermen stand on the riverbank and all of a sudden there it is, in the water—the black inside the eye. Shining.

Everything that shines also sees.

Poplars cast their shadows down the stairs along the riverbank, the shadows break up on the steps and do not enter the water. When the streetcar crosses the bridge, new shadows push the smaller ones out into the current, just like the dictator's forelock pushes his smaller curls to the back of his head.

Poplar light mixes with poplar shade until the whole city is covered in stripes. Stone slabs, walls, clumps of grass, river and banks.

No one is walking by the water, even though it's a summer day, a summer practically made for strolling aimlessly along the river.

The fishermen don't trust the striped summer. They know the poplar shadows on the ground are the same thing as the poplars in the sky, knives.

Fish won't come anywhere near that, say the fishermen. When a dark stripe from the poplars falls on the fishing rods, the men move to sunnier grass and cast their lines into a brighter patch of water.

A woman walks along the river, carrying a pillow tied up with string. She carries it in front of her, cradling it in both arms, the wind is beating from behind. Perhaps there's a child inside, a sleeping infant with two heads, one on each end, where the strings have more slack. The woman's arms are brown, but her calves are as white as the pillow. One of the fishermen eyes her calves. Her buttocks sway as she walks. The fisherman's gaze falls into the water, wearied and shriveled by the poplars' headstand. His eyes detect the slightest hint of evening. In the middle of the day it sneaks down the ridge of his nose. His fingers pull a cigarette from his pocket and hold it to his lips. The fire flares at one corner of his mouth, his hand grows big and covers the flame, the wind is picking up.

The fishermen cast their lines into the river and pull out drowned grass, decaying socks and waterlogged underpants. And once a day, when the rods are bent and the lines drunk from imbibing the river bottom, an oily fish. Or maybe a dead cat.

Even the tiniest touch of evening felt on the ridge of their noses steals everything. And what it can't steal, it forbids. Including happiness, say the fishermen. The striped summer takes all the joy out of fishing.

The poplars are full of pods that are neither fruit nor seed but galls, misshapen thimbles for flies and aphids. The bugs drop out of the poplars surrounding the café and crawl across the newspaper. Adina's fingertips shove them into the dictator's forelock, the flies crawl along his ear hairs, the aphids feel the bright glossy shine and play dead.

The waitress lowers the tray, sees the face on the table, her cheekbones twitch, her ears burn. She averts her eyes so quickly that a blue vein of fear snaps across her temples as she sets the glass right on top of the dictator's forehead. The lemonade is thinly streaked with yellow swirls, the forelock appears inside the glass. Adina clinks her spoon, the spoon shines, the lemonade shines, everything that shines also sees. A hot needle of light flashes across her forehead, the streetcar passes over the bridge, setting off waves in the river. Adina leaves her spoon in her drink, she doesn't touch the glass and lets her hand rest just like the spoon. Adina is waiting for Clara and Paul. She turns her head away.

Beyond the flat roof of the café is the park, beyond the park the rooftops are pointed. Here are the streets of the directors and inspectors, the mayors, secret police and army officers. The quiet streets of power, where even the wind is afraid when it starts to blow. And when it does blow it is afraid to eddy. And when it blusters it would rather break its own ribs than a branch. Dry leaves scratch across the walkways, quickly covering all tracks. If someone sets foot on these streets who does not live on one of them, who does not belong, it is for these streets as though nothing was there.

The quiet streets of power abide in the breeze that forks the branches in the park and festoons them with leaves and picks up their rustling, the breeze that carries the clatter of footsteps along the river path, the breeze that causes people on both banks to lift their feet when they walk across the grass, even if it's mowed, and raise their knees into their throats. Those who come here on foot prefer to pass unnoticed, with high, slow steps. Meanwhile inside their throats they are running, rushing. Once they reach the bridge, the city cloaks them in mindless noise, and they can breathe more easily, as the streetcar whooshes by, tugging their heads out of the silence.

The masters of the quiet streets are never seen in their houses or gardens. Behind the fir trees, servants come and go up and down the stone steps. When they walk on the lawn, they draw their insides into their throats for fear of squashing the grass. When they cut the grass, a mirror appears in the whites of their eyes, where sickles and rakes gleam like scissors and combs. The servants don't trust their own skins, because whenever they reach for something their hands cast a shadow. Their heads know that they were born with dirty hands in dirty streets, and that their hands will never grow clean here in the silence. Only old. The clock ticks on the wall, the curtains billow, and when the servants open their masters' refrigerators and look inside, a square of light falls on their feet, their eyes are startled, and their cheeks shiver at the thoughts that pass through their minds. The meat is packed in cellophane, the cellophane is coated with frost, the frost is white like stone, like the marble in the garden.

In the gardens of the quiet streets there are no gnomes with caps. Nothing but sad, barefoot stones. Naked lions, white as snow-covered dogs, and naked wingless angels, like snow-covered children. Yet even here, when the winter proceeds along its orbit around the sun, the snow crusts yellow and breaks without melting.

The servants live in the cellars underneath the houses, more likely to brush against pill bugs and mice than if they lived on the floorboards overhead. The servants' husbands are all lying in the earth, the servants' children have all left home. The servants are widows.

One of the servants has a daughter who teaches at the same school as Adina. And one day when they were walking by the river the daughter said, my mother works in the yellow house behind the round garden. And she raised her hand over her head and pointed out a house on the other side. Her eyes were dull, or perhaps her gaze was simply frozen, because the day was so cold and the water so close. She giggled as they crossed the bridge, then a streetcar passed and quashed the giggling. In the evening, said the servant's daughter, when it's already dark, the master of the house comes back from the Military Casino at Freedom Square, he's an officer and spends his days there drinking. In the evening he doesn't so much find his way back home as it finds him. Before he leaves, the waitresses put his officer's cap on his head backward. So he teeters through the streets with the visor sticking out in back, until the way finds him. And every evening when he gets home, said the servant's daughter, he and his wife go through the same ritual: DANUBE DELTA. The cathedral bell interrupted the servant's daughter, she looked up and burst into laughter, the bell's chiming clung to her lips. From the reflection in the display windows Adina once again sensed how close they were to the water. The servant's daughter bent over to check her shoes, Adina could see the soles mirrored in her eyes. I don't like these heels, the servant's daughter said. She made a face and said DANUBE DELTA, and resumed her story.

When the officer has made it home, his wife can hear his boots scraping up the steps between the lions. She says to my mother: DANUBE DELTA. My mother fetches a pot of hot water from the kitchen, which she carries to the bathroom and pours into a basin set on the floor. Then she tops it off with cold water so it's nice and lukewarm. The officer's wife waits in the front hall. Before her husband can turn the key, she opens the door from inside. She takes the briefcase out of his hand and the cap off his head and says DANUBE DELTA. The officer mutters and nods. His wife heads for the bathroom, he follows, by the time he gets there his wife is already perched on the closed toilet seat. The officer removes his boots and sets them outside the door. His wife says, let's see your stork. The officer undresses and hands her his uniform, she folds the pants and drapes them over her arm. He takes off his underpants, spreads his legs and crouches so that he's straddling the basin, then lowers himself to his knees and gazes at the blue tiles above the mirror. His penis dangles in the water. If his testicles sink, his wife says, good. If they float, she bursts into tears and screams, you've fucked yourself empty, even your boots are limp. The officer sinks his face between his knees, looks at his floating testicles and says, I swear my love, I swear.

The servant's daughter stared for a moment at the leafless shrub brushing against her coat and said, my mother doesn't know what it is he swears, meanwhile the mirror fogs up and the man keeps swearing. Then, long after his wife is quiet, he starts to cry. With him it's just a yammer, with her it's more. My mother sits in her place in the living room, at the long end of the table, facing the bathroom, ashamed to the back of her eyes. She hides her hands under the table because they're shaking. If she so much as moves her slipper, the woman says, Lenuza, you stay put. And to the officer she says, now stick your stork back in your pants. The man stands up and puts on his underwear. His wife carries his pants on her arm through the living room, always clinging first to the edge of the table, then to my mother's shoulder. She says, Lenuza, clean up, then her hand goes back to the table and follows it like a guardrail over to the bedroom door. Her husband traipses after her, boots in hand. And my mother cleans up the bathroom and switches off the light.

The servant's daughter blew warm breath onto her hands. My coat doesn't have any pockets, she said, it came from the officer's wife. She rubbed her fingers on her coat, hitting the buttons with her nails, a sound like stones hitting stones.

I have a hard time believing the whole business, said the servant's daughter. But my mother's never lied before. She hears them behind the bedroom door, the officer snores and his wife hums:

Roses in bloom
Come again soon
Lovely once more
Roses in bloom

My mother knows the song, the woman sings it in the kitchen every day. My mother walks on her tiptoes but the floorboards creak. The wife can tell when my mother is by the front door ready to lock up and then she says, don't forget to lock up twice Lenuza. The wife is afraid of the stone angel, that it might enter the house during the night. That's why she has her lions. Now and then the wife says to my mother, his angel can't get past my two lions. The officer bought the angel to ward against his wife's lions. But my mother says the lions and the angel won't hurt each other because they all come from the same stonecutter. The officer realizes that, said the servant's daughter, but his wife doesn't.

In the morning, when the officer is in his cap and boots, his wife stands in the hall and brushes his uniform jacket. He bends down slowly to pick up his briefcase, she bends down with him and keeps brushing. The brush is so small that at first my mother couldn't see it in the wife's hand. My mother wondered why she crooked her hand when she stroked her husband's jacket. Then one time the woman dropped the brush. Her hands are so small, until that moment my mother thought they weren't capable of hiding anything. The officer's wife is very tall, said the servant's daughter, I've never seen hands that small on such a tall woman. After the officer leaves, his wife watches him through the window. Two houses later she loses sight of him but she waits until he reemerges, first at the entrance to the bridge and then once more on the bridge itself. The woman says she's more worried something might happen to her husband when he's sober, in the morning while he's crossing the bridge, than on his way back home.

Then there's the story with the perfume flask, said the servant's daughter. The wife carries it stashed in her purse, even though the flask has been empty for years. The bottle has a rose etched into the glass, and a stopper that used to be gold-plated, by now the plating has worn off, but you can still see a few Cyrillic letters engraved on the side—it must have been Russian perfume. Years ago a Russian officer was in the house, but no one ever mentions him. He had blue eyes. Occasionally the wife says that the handsomest officers have blue eyes. Her husband has brown eyes and occasionally says to his wife, I see you're reeking of roses again. The servant's daughter slowly moistened her lower lip with the tip of her tongue. There must be something special about that flask, she said, something sad. Something that opens a wish and closes a door, because it's not her husband's absence that makes her so lonely, it's the empty perfume bottle in her purse. Sometimes, she said, her mother feels the woman's head is sinking farther and farther into her neck, as if a staircase were running from her throat to her ankle and she were climbing down the steps carrying her own head. Perhaps because my mother lives in the cellar, said the servant's daughter. The officer's wife spends half the day sitting at the table, and her eyes are piercingly empty, like dried-out sunflower disks. The servant's daughter wiped her nose, rubbing her red nostrils with a crumpled handkerchief, then stuffed the handkerchief back in her purse like a snowball. She explained that every year the officer's wife buys her mother a pair of genuine lambskin gloves, and every week she gives her coffee beans and Russian tea.

But because my mother scrimps and saves, said the servant's daughter, she always gives me the tea and coffee. She can't give me the gloves, though, otherwise the officer's wife would notice. She did manage to have the ones from the year before last disappear by claiming that the postman's dog had gotten hold of them and chewed them up so much they were no longer fit to wear. The postman denied it but he couldn't prove anything.

The servant's daughter told Adina that her mother had also gotten her the job at the school, thanks to the officer's wife.

Two fishermen are standing next to each other on the riverbank. One of them takes off his cap, his hair is packed down, the band has left a ring pressed into the back of his head. Underneath one cap he has another—a cap of white hair. The other man is eating sunflower seeds and spitting out the husks, they float on the river, white inside and black outside. He holds out a handful to the man with the white cap of hair and says, take some to pass the time. The man brushes them away. They're too much like melon seeds, he says. When I came back from the front, everything they ate here at home was like one big cemetery. Sausage, cheese, bread, even milk and cucumbers were all buried under lids or shut away behind a cupboard door, just like a grave. Now, after all these years I don't know. He bends down, picks up a small rock, turns it over in his hand and shuts his right eye. He flings the rock into the river so that it skips four times, dancing on the water before it sinks. I no longer feel the same disgust, he says, but I'm still afraid of the insides of melons because they remind me of coffins. The fisherman with the sunflower seeds lowers his head, his mouth is narrow, his eyes skewed. He moves both rods to sunnier grass.

The sun is high in the sky, on top of the city. The rods cast shadows, the afternoon leans against the shadows. As soon as the day tips over, Adina thinks, and the sunlight goes skidding away, it will cut deep trenches in the fields around the city and the corn will snap in two.

When they don't speak, the fishermen don't move. If they aren't talking with each other, they're not alive. Their silence has no reason, the words simply falter. The clock inside the cathedral tower advances, the bell chimes, another hour is empty and gone, it could be today, it could be tomorrow. Nobody on the banks of the river hears the chiming, the sound quiets when it reaches the water and whimpers until it's gone.

The fishermen measure the day by the heat of the sky and can tell by looking at the smoke above the wire factory if it's raining elsewhere. And by feeling the burn on their shoulders they can sense how long the sun will keep growing and when it will sink and shatter.

Anyone who truly knows the river has seen heaven from the inside, say the fishermen. As the city starts getting dark, there's a moment when the clock in the tower can no longer measure time. Its face turns white and casts a sheen into the park. When that happens, the fine-toothed acacia leaves look like combs. The clock hands skip ahead, but the evening refuses to believe what they're saying. The white sheen does not last long.

But while it does last, all the fishermen lie down beside one another on their stomachs and gaze into the river. And during that time, say the fishermen, the river shows anyone who truly knows it a foul, rotten gullet. That is heaven from the inside. The gullet is in the middle of the current, not on the river bottom. It holds so many clothes that they reach from one bridge to the other. The gullet itself is naked, it holds the clothes in its hands. They are the clothes of the drowned, say the fishermen.

The fishermen don't stare at the gullet for long, after a few brief glances most lay their faces in the grass and laugh so hard their legs shake. But the fisherman with the white cap of hair doesn't laugh. When the others ask why his legs are shaking even though he isn't laughing, he says, when I lay my face in the grass, I see my own brain, naked in the water.

A Gypsy boy is standing inside the café next to the table farthest in back. He holds an empty beer glass over his face, the foam trickles down in a thread, his mouth swallows before the foam reaches his lips. Stop that, says Adina out loud, you're drinking with your forehead, like you don't have a mouth. Then the boy is at her table, give me a leu he says, holding his hand out over the newspaper. Adina sets a coin down next to the glass, the boy covers it with his hand and drags it off the table. May God keep you beautiful and good, he says. And though he speaks of God, all Adina sees of his face in the sunlight are two whitish-yellow eyes. Have some lemonade, she says.

A fly is swimming in the glass, he fishes it out with a spoon, blows it onto the ground and stashes the spoon in his pocket.

Shoshoi, the waitress yells.

The boy's throat is dry, a gurgling comes from inside his shirt. He raises the glass and drains it in one gulp, through his face and all the way to his whitish-yellow eyes. He stashes the glass in his pocket as well.

Shoshoi, the waitress screams.

Clara once explained that shoshoi in Romani means HARE, that Gypsies are afraid of hares. It's more that they're afraid of superstitions, said Paul, and as a result they're always afraid.

Once, he went on, an elderly Gypsy was being discharged from the hospital. Paul jotted down what the man was allowed to eat. But the man didn't know how to read. So Paul read the list out loud, including the word HARE. I cannot take this piece of paper, the man said. You are a gentleman, you have to write out another one. Paul scratched through the word HARE, the man shook his head. That won't do, he said, it's still there. You may be a doctor but you are not a gentleman. You don't understand how your own heart beats inside you. Inside the hare beats the heart of the earth, that's why we are Gypsies, because we understand that, sir, that's why we're always on the run.

The Gypsy boy dashes off, the poplar stripes slice him as he runs, his soles fly up to his back as splashes of white. The waitress chases after the soles. The fisherman with the sunflower seeds watches the splashing soles. Like gravel hitting water, he says.

The wind blows in the brush, the boy's eyes lurk among the leaves. The waitress stands in the grass, panting, alert, the leaves fan back and forth, she doesn't see the boy. The waitress lets her head droop, removes her sandals and slowly heads back through the poplar stripes to the café, stepping barefoot in small strides over the stone slabs. The shadows from her sandals dangle below her hand. The shadows don't reveal how high the heels are or how thin the laces, or how the buckles sparkle once just beneath her ring and again on the stone. The fisherman with the sunflower seeds says in her direction, with those legs you'd be better off running after me. Without shoes look how sturdy they are, take off those high heels and you're a peasant woman.

The fisherman who's afraid of melons scratches his crotch and says, once during the war I wound up in this small village. I've forgotten the name. I looked through a window and saw a woman at a sewing machine. She was sewing a white lace curtain, the cloth was spilling over onto the floor. I knocked and said WATER. She came to the door, dragging her curtain with her. The water bucket had a ladle, I drank one ladleful after another. I was only looking at the water, but in the water I could see her bare calves, all pudgy and white. The water was cold and the roof of my mouth was hot, my throat was pounding in my ears. The woman pulled me to the floor, she wasn't wearing anything underneath her dress. The lace scratched, and her stomach had no bottom. She didn't say a word. I often think about the fact I never heard her voice. I didn't say anything either. Not until I was back on the street did I say to myself, WATER.

The fisherman with the sunflower seeds bites a thread off the hem of his shirt and says, it all depends on the calves. When I'm on top of my wife she complains the neighbors are going to pound on the wall in the middle of the night and call out, stop beating her. There's nothing behind the complaining, I've known for a long time that everything under her nightshirt has gone cold, only her mouth screams. I lie on top of her and get used to the dark, I see her wide open eyes, her forehead way up high, looking grayish yellow like the moon, and her sagging chin. I see her twisting her mouth. I could use my nose and peck her right in her gaping eyes but I don't. She groans like someone trying to move a wardrobe, not like someone who enjoys it. Her ribs are so hard that her heart's all withered up inside, and her legs are getting thinner every day. She doesn't have any meat on her calves. All the flesh on her body goes to her stomach, which is growing rounder and rounder and spreading out like a fat sheep.

The fisherman takes off one shoe, turns it over, shakes out a cherry pit. Sometimes the moon shines between the ceiling and the wall of our room, he says, so the moonlight has a crease, and I can see the pattern of the wineglasses in the cabinet and the fringe of the carpet. My eyes trace the fringe of the carpet as I let the day pass through my head. The fisherman with the cap of white hair plucks a grass straw and sticks it in his mouth. As he chews the straw wags back and forth. But letting the day pass through your head—the poplars, the river—doesn't take very long, says the fisherman with the sunflower seeds. Today I have the waitress to think about so tonight it will last longer.

The fisherman with the grass straw laughs, and says, and the Gypsy. Tonight it will last longer, says the fisherman with the sunflower seeds, and I'll take even longer to fall asleep. You know, every night I can hear the crickets outside. The whole bed shakes each time the nightshirt turns over. The crickets chirp, they pull one long note like a dark string, they eat up all my peace and quiet. I sense that they could be right underneath our room, so I hold my breath. I have the feeling they're carrying our entire apartment block on their backs through the grass, across the long flat plain, all the way to the Danube. When I fall asleep I dream I'm stepping out of the apartment onto the street. But there isn't any street and I'm standing there barefoot in my pajamas, next to the water, freezing. I have to escape, I have to flee across the Danube to Yugoslavia. And I don't know how to swim.

On the other side of the river two men are sitting on a bench. Both are wearing suits. The sunlight shines right through their ears, which look like leaves next to each other. One wears a tie flecked with reddish blue. At the end of the bench is a patch of shadow that could be a coat, without sleeves, without a collar, without pockets, it's no longer there when the light moves to the next branch. Both men are eating sunflower seeds. The husks fly quickly into the water. The wind moves the branch, the coat shrinks.

The fisherman with the white cap of hair glances toward the two men, then spits out the grass straw. Do you know those two birds over there, he asks. Anyway I really don't know how to swim, says the fisherman with the sunflower seeds. He shrugs his shoulders and continues quietly.

There was this one dream about the Danube, he says, which my wife was also in. When I reached the water she was already there. She didn't recognize me. She asked me the way you'd ask a stranger, are you trying to make it across the border too? She was leaving the gravel bank, heading away from the water. There were willows and hazelnut bushes. The current's strong, she called out, I have to eat something first. She went rummaging through the underbrush, but there was nothing except river grass, so she picked through the branches and tore the hazelnuts off together with the stems and leaves. The hazelnuts weren't ripe, they still had their green outer shells. So she pounded them with a round stone. She ate, and a milky liquid flowed from her mouth. I looked away, into the water. Our Father who art in Heaven and on Earth. The words came out of my mouth like the pounding from the stone. I couldn't pray anymore, I felt foolish. The Lord was listening to the stone and the hazelnuts, not to me. I turned to her and screamed so loud my voice stung my eyes, I can't do it, come back here to me, I can't make it across, I tell you I don't know how to swim.

An aphid settles on the dictator's forehead and plays dead.

Adina often comes to this café, because it overlooks the river, because every year the park grows longer by the length of an arm, and because the new growth on the trees stays soft and bright even late in the summer. And because she can look at the old branches and see the past year still swaying. The bark is dark and tough, the leaves coarsely ribbed, summer won't be over anytime soon. The frost doesn't come until October. Then it cuts down the leaves in a single night, as though some major accident occurred.

The breath of fear looms in the park, it slows the mind and makes people see their lives in everything others say and do. No one ever knows if a given thought will become a spoken sentence or a knot in the throat. Or merely the flaring of nostrils, in and out.

The breath of fear sharpens hearing.

At the wire factory, smoke flies out of the chimneys and frays until all that's left are the summer old folk floating over the city. And the clothes in the rotten gullet of the river down below.

Once Adina has gotten used to the breath of fear, she can feel her knee as something separate from the wrought-iron chair. The quiet streets of power hitch themselves to the streetcar crossing the bridge over the river. And they're drawn from their quiet neighborhood into the center of the city, into the outskirts of town, into the filthy streets of the servants. Where it's clear from the dried mud that all the children have left home and all the husbands are lying in the earth. The gaps in the windows are sealed with old newspapers, and the widows have fled with outstretched arms to the streets of power.

If a person sits long enough in the café, the fear settles down and waits. And the next day it's already right there at the same table. It's an aphid inside your head that won't crawl away. If a person sits too long the fear just plays dead.

Clara lifts her dress as she joggles the chair, she's just shaved her legs, her skin is so smooth it's freckled red at every pore. Yesterday Mara had to count spools of wire, she says, and today the director called her into his office. He stood by the window and counted the spools again himself. After he'd finished he said, you have legs like a deer. Mara turned red and said thank you. And the director said, I mean as hairy as a deer's.

Four women are rowing on the water, their arm muscles swell and bulge. A fifth woman holds a megaphone to her mouth, she shouts into the cone across the water, without looking at the rowers.

Clara passes through the poplar stripes on her way into town. Her shoes clatter along the river. The forelock sees the shouts from the megaphone as they land in between Clara's steps.

The fisherman with the white cap of hair whistles a song.

The man with the reddish-blue flecked tie gets up off the bench. As he walks he spits a sunflower husk into the river, and combs his hair while climbing the steps. He stands on the bridge, then sets off in pursuit of Clara's legs, her flying summer dress. As he walks he lights a cigarette.

Paul hands Adina a white envelope and holds the newspaper in front of his face, the nail on one thumb is torn. The skin on his index finger is yellow, he's smoked so much it's growing a tobacco leaf. Adina opens the envelope, it's from Liviu, a wedding invitation with two interlocking rings.

Liviu is a schoolmate of Paul's who for the past two years has been teaching in a small village in the south, in the part of the country cut off by the Danube, where the fields bump against the sky and the withered thistles toss their white fluff into the river. The farmers in the village drink plum brandy before breakfast, before heading out to the field, Liviu said. And the women force-feed the geese with fattened maize. And the policeman, the pastor, the mayor and the teacher all have gold teeth in their mouths.

The Romanian farmers eat and drink too much because they have too little, said Liviu, and they talk too little because they know too much. And they don't trust strangers even if they eat and drink the exact same things, because strangers don't have any gold teeth. Strangers here are very much alone, said Liviu.

That's why Liviu is marrying a teacher from the village, a woman who belongs.

As good as a piece of bread

A man whistles a song as he leads his horse down the side of the road. The song is slower than his own steps, and the horse's gait does not throw off his timing. As he walks the man keeps his eyes on the ground. The dust every morning is older than the day.

Adina can feel the song in the soles of her feet, the man sings straight from his mouth into her head:

The worries refuse to leave me alone
Must I sell my field and my house and my home

A short man, a thin rope, a big horse.

A thin rope for a horse is a thick rope for a man. A man with a rope is a hanged man. Like the tinsmith from the outskirts of town.

On a day like every day, when the streetcar rolled past his display window with the stovepipes, grave crosses and watering cans the way it always did, the tinsmith was a hanged man.

The passengers hovered behind the streetcar windows, each holding a lamb because it was almost Easter.

The fire had stopped chewing his pots, but death didn't bite the tinsmith in the ass the way he always said. Instead, it squashed his neck.

His few fingers had taken a rope and made a noose. It was the man from the slaughterhouse who found him, the one who'd thrown the barber's cat out the door. He had ordered a stovepipe from the tinsmith and went to pick it up. He was coming from the barber. His hair was freshly cut, and his chin was freshly shaved, he smelled of grass oil. Lavender was what the barber called it, but all the men the barber shaved had shiny faces and smelled like grass.

When the man who smelled like grass found the hanged tinsmith he said, such a good craftsman and such shoddy work.

Because the tinsmith was hanging all askew, right next to the door, and his body was so close to the floor he could have stood on his tiptoes and stepped out of the noose had he wanted to.

The man who smelled like grass reached over the hanged man's head and said, pity to waste a good piece of rope, so instead of cutting the rope, he loosened the noose. The hanged man tumbled out, and his leather apron folded as he fell, but he himself did not. When his shoulder hit the ground, his head stayed straight. The man who smelled like grass then untied the knot and coiled the rope, drawing it between his thumb and forefinger and across his palm and over his elbow. When he tied off the short end he said, this rope will come in handy in the slaughterhouse.

The seamstress came in and stashed a pair of pliers and a new shiny nail in her apron pocket. She lowered her head, her tears dripped onto the alarm clock sitting on the table, as the locomotive pictured on the timepiece ticked away. The seamstress looked at the hands on the dial and reached for a watering can, I'll take that for tending his grave, she said. And the man who smelled like grass said, I don't know. He searched around for his stovepipe.

And the barber said, the tinsmith came by my place just an hour ago, I gave him a shave. His face was still wet and he went and hanged himself. The barber pocketed a small file into his smock. He looked at the man who smelled like grass and said, whoever cuts down a hanged man fashions his own noose. The man who smelled like grass had three stovepipes tucked under his arm, he showed the barber the rope, look here, nothing's been cut.

Adina saw a mountain of soldered pots on the floor next to the hanged man. The enamel was chipped and stained. Parsley and lovage, onion and garlic, tomatoes and cucumbers. A clove, a slice, a leaf, everything that summer coaxed out of the earth had left its mark. The vegetables of gardens and fields on the outskirts of every town, and the meat of all the yards and stalls.

When the doctor came everyone took a step away from the tinsmith, as if the horror were only just arriving. Silence twisted every face, as though the doctor were bringing death itself.

The doctor undressed the tinsmith and examined the pots. Tugging on the lifeless hands he said, how can a person solder with just three fingers on each hand. When the doctor dropped the tinsmith's pants onto the floor two apricots fell out of the pocket. They were round and smooth, the same yellow as the soldering flame that no longer chewed the pots. The apricots raced under the table, glowing as they went.

The string hung around the neck of the tinsmith as it always did, but the wedding ring had disappeared.

For several days and nights the air under the trees had a bitter smell. Adina saw the empty string in the veins of whitewashed walls and in the cracks of asphalt streets. The first afternoon she suspected the seamstress, and that first evening she suspected the man who smelled like grass. The next day she suspected the barber and in the night, which sank into the evening without any twilight, she suspected the doctor.

Two days after the tinsmith hanged himself, Adina's mother crossed the beet fields to the village with the sheep, whose gleaming white walls could be seen from the outskirts of town. Because it was almost Easter, she bought a lamb. The women in the village told Adina's mother that a child nobody had ever seen before had been at the tinsmith's and stolen the ring right off his neck. The tinsmith's ring was gold and could have been sold to pay for a funeral pall. As it was, the money in his worktable drawer barely paid for a rough narrow box. That's not a coffin, said the women, it's a wooden suit.

The man leading the horse stops at the edge of town and is hidden for a moment by a passing bus. Then the bus is gone, the man stands in the dust, and the horse walks around him. The man steps over the halter, slings it around a tree trunk and ties it off tight. At the shop he pushes through the door and makes his way past the waiting heads to join the bread line.

Before he disappears among the screaming heads, the man glances back. The horse lifts its hooves and stands on three legs for longer than it takes a bus to pass, then rubs its flank against the tree trunk.

Adina feels dust in her eye. The horse's head becomes a blur sniffing at the tree bark. The dust in Adina's eye is a tiny fly on her fingertip. The horse munches on a branch, the acacia leaves rustle beneath his muzzle, the scraggy wood has thorns and crackles in his throat.

Warm air spills onto the street from the store where the man disappeared. The buses kick up great wheels of dust in their wake. The sun hitches a ride with every bus, fluttering on the corners like an open shirt. The morning smells of gasoline and dust and worn-out shoes. And when someone passes by carrying bread, the sidewalk smells of hunger.

Hunger sharpens elbows for shoving and teeth for screaming. The shop has fresh bread. The elbows inside the shop are countless, but the bread is counted.

Where the dust flies highest the street is narrow, the apartment buildings crooked and jammed together. The grass grows thick along the pathways, and when it blooms, brash and brazen, it's always tattered by the wind. The more brazen the spikes, the greater the poverty. Here summer threshes itself, mistaking torn clothing for chaff. The eyes lurking at the windows matter as much to the gleaming panes as the flying seeds to the grass.

Children pluck grass straws with milky stems out of the earth and make a game of sucking them dry. And in their play is hunger. Their lungs cease to grow, the grass milk feeds their dirty fingers and the wart clusters, but not their baby teeth, which fall out. The teeth don't wiggle long, they drop into the children's hands while they're talking. The children toss them over their shoulders and behind their backs into the grass, today one, tomorrow another. As each tooth flies, they shout:

Mouse o mouse bring me a brand-new tooth,
And you can have my old one.

Only after the tooth has disappeared in the grass do they look back and call it childhood.

The mouse takes the teeth and lines its burrows under the apartment building with little white tiles. It does not bring the children new teeth.

The school is located at the bottom of the street, at the top of the street is a broken phone booth. The balconies on the buildings in between are made of rusty corrugated sheet metal and can't hold anything more than a few tired geraniums and a little laundry fluttering from a line. And clematis, which climbs high and attaches itself to the rust.

No dahlias bloom here, where everything is rusting and breaking and falling apart, and where the clematis unravels its own summer, blue and hypocritical, saving its most beautiful blooms for the rubble.

At the top of the street the clematis creeps into the broken phone booth, it lies down on the glass splinters but does not get cut. It twines around the dial and stops it from spinning.

The one-eyed numbers on the dial pronounce their own names when Adina passes slowly by: one, two, three.

A fool's summer during marches, a soldier's summer beyond the long plain in the south. Ilie is wearing a uniform. In his mouth he has a straw of summer grass, and in his pocket a calendar with a winter full of crossed-out days. And a picture of Adina. On the plain are a hill, a wall, and the barracks. The grass straw comes from the hill, wrote Ilie on the back of the picture.

Whenever Adina sees tall grass, she thinks about Ilie and looks for his face. In her head she carries a mailbox. Whenever she opens it, the box is empty, Ilie seldom writes letters. Writing letters makes me remember where I am, he wrote. Paul said, people seldom write letters when they know for sure that they are loved.

For as long as the clematis was green, a man lay in the telephone booth. His forehead was so short that his hair began right above his eyebrows. Because his forehead's so empty, said the passersby, because his brain's made of brandy and brandy evaporates, and when it does there's nothing left.

The man lay in the booth, and his shoes rested on their heels. Anyone walking by could see the soles but not the shoes. The man drank and talked out loud to himself when he wasn't sleeping. People sped up when they came to the booth, and kept a distance from its shadow. They clutched their hair as though not to lose their thoughts. They spit absentmindedly on the sidewalk or into the grass because their mouths had a bitter taste. When the man talked to himself out loud, the passersby averted their eyes, and when he slept, some ventured closer to kick the soles of his shoes with the tips of theirs until he groaned. None of them ever wanted to rouse a corpse, but each of them hoped that day had come.

A bottle was propped against the man's stomach, his fingers were around the neck, he held the bottle firmly, and didn't loosen his grip even in his sleep.

Until one day the man did loosen his grip, and the bottle fell over. A woman kicked the soles of his shoes. After that the caretaker came from the nearest apartment building, then a child, then a policeman. The man in the phone booth no longer groaned, his death smelled of plum brandy.

The caretaker tossed the dead man's empty bottle into the grass and said, if there really is such a thing as a soul then his was in that bottle and it was the last thing he swallowed. And that means that his soul is whatever his stomach didn't manage to digest. The policeman whistled and stopped a horse cart on the street. The driver set down his whip and climbed out. He lifted the dead man by the arms while the caretaker lifted him by the shoes. They carried the stiff weight through the sun like a board, then they swung the board onto the cart, on top of the green cabbage heads. The driver covered the dead man with a horse blanket and picked up his whip. He tapped the horse and clicked his tongue, twisting his mouth.

The phone booth still smells of plum brandy, and for two days the wind has been making a different sound in the street. The clematis has kept growing and blooming, blue as ever, the one-eyed numbers stare from the dial. Adina dials in her head and talks to the dead man until she's left the phone booth well behind.

I'm at the other end of the line, he says.

You're skin and bones, she says, you're just a board.

Doesn't matter, he says, I'm a whole person, half crazy and half drunk.

Show me your hands, she says.

Wine in the mouth, cognac in the stomach, brandy in the brain, he says.

She sees his shoes, he drinks standing up.

Stop, she says, you're drinking with your forehead, like you don't have a mouth.

Near the bottom of the street a large spool of wire is rusting away. The grass around it is yellow. Behind the spool is a fence, behind the fence is a yard and a wooden shack. In the yard a dog jerks on his chain, pulling it across the grass. The dog never barks.

No one knows what the dog is guarding. Early in the morning and late in the evening, always after dark, policemen come. They talk to the dog, feed him, and light their cigarettes but do not finish them. According to the children from the apartments there are three policemen. Because their rooms have only candles, the children can see three cigarettes smoldering outside the wooden shack. Their mothers pull them away from the windows. The dog is named Olga, according to the children, but the dog is male, not female.

The dog looks at Adina every day, its eyes mirror the grass. Every day Adina says OLGA, so the dog won't bark.

Yellow leaves lie strewn on the grass beneath the poplars in front of the school, which change color long before the poplars in town do. And in March the poplars in front of the school turn green, before all the other poplars in the city. The poplars in front of the school have a mind of their own. The teachers claim this is because the school is on the edge of town, with no protection from the weather coming off the open fields. The director says the leaves turn yellow so early because the children piss on the trunks, like dogs.

But really the poplars by the school turn yellow so early because of the factory where women make red chamber pots and green clothespins. The women who work there cough and turn barren, and the poplars turn yellow. Even in summer the women wear thick knee-length underwear with elastic bands. Every day they pad their legs and stomachs with clothespins, sticking so many in their underwear that nothing rattles when they walk. In the center of town, on the plaza by the opera, the women's children loop strings of clothespins over their shoulders and trade them for panty hose, cigarettes or soap. In the winter the women hide whole chamber pots full of clothespins in their underwear. Nothing can be seen beneath their coats.

The bell rings across the school yard and through the poplars. No one is walking through the yard, no one is hurrying through the halls. No class is about to begin. The children are sitting on a truck under the poplars in front of the school. They are being driven far past the city, out to the tomatoes ripening in the field.

Their shoes are sticky with bits of squashed tomato from yesterday, the day before, whole weeks from morning to evening. Their pockets are sticky with squashed tomato, as are their water bottles, their jackets and shirts and pants. Also with grass seed, nightshade, and withered clumps of thistle fluff.

Thistle fluff is for the pillows of the dead, say the mothers, when their children return home late from the fields. Machine oil eats away at the skin, they say, but thistle fluff devours the mind. They stroke their children's hair for several moments, and then, without warning, they slap them in the face. After that both children and mothers stare in silence at the candlelight. The eyes are full of guilt, but this can't be seen by the light of the candles.

Dust sticks to the children's hair, it makes their heads stubborn and their hair kinked, their eyelashes short and their eyes hard. The children on the truck don't talk much. They look at the poplars and eat the fresh bread that has been counted. Their wart-clustered fingers are quick and nimble, the first thing they do is bore a hole in the crust. The children eat the inside first. It's white and unbaked, the dough has scarcely been numbed by the heat of the oven, it sticks to their teeth. The children chew and say they are eating the HEART. They soften the crust with spit and form it into hats, noses and ears. This leaves their fingers tired and their mouths empty.

The driver closes the tailgate. His shirt is missing a button, so the steering wheel touches his navel. Four loaves of bread are lying on the dashboard. Next to the steering wheel is the picture of a blond Serbian singer. A streetcar comes too close, the bread scrapes against the windshield, the driver curses, mother of all streetcars.

Far past the city is not a direction. Wheat stubble without end, until the eyes can no longer make out its pale color. Only the undergrowth and the dust on the leaves.

The harvesters are pretty big, says the driver, and that's a good thing because when you're perched up there in the seat you can't see the dead bodies lying in the wheat field. His throat is covered with hair, his Adam's apple is a mouse hopping between his shirt and his chin. The wheat's pretty high, too, he says, high enough that you can't see the soldiers' dogs, just their eyes. Except it's not high enough to hide the people trying to sneak across the border. Adina grips her knees tightly, they pass a bird sitting in a rosebush by the edge of the field and pecking at a hip on the topmost branch. A red kite, says the driver. You know, when they say GOD'S ACRE they mean the cemetery. I spent three summers running the harvester near the border, all by myself on the field at harvesttime, and then two winters plowing, only at night. The field has a sweet kind of stink, when you think about it GOD'S ACRE really ought to mean a wheat field. They say a good person is as good as a piece of bread, at least that's what the teachers teach the children.

The red kite sits motionless on the field as though its belly were impaled on the stubble. The sky sees that the stubble field is empty and hard and that the bird's belly is soft, and rolls out two white clouds while the stubble sucks the bird's belly dry. The driver's eyes twitch in the corners, the blackthorn is studded with bluish green spheres and isn't afraid of the bus wheels.

But you can't tell children that a person is as good as a piece of bread, says the driver, otherwise they'll believe it and won't be able to grow anymore. And you can't tell that to old people either, they can sense when you're lying and then they'll shrink until they're as small as the children because they never forget anything. His Adam's apple hops from his chin into his shirt. My wife and I, he says, the only time we talk is at night, when we can't sleep. My wife wants to be good, so she doesn't buy bread. The driver laughs, the potholes jerk his gaze onto the field, but I end up buying it anyway, he says. We eat it and like it, my wife too. She eats and cries and is getting older and fat. She's a better person than me, but who's really good these days. When she can't bear it anymore instead of screaming she goes to throw up. He tucks his shirt in his pants. She vomits quietly, so the neighbors don't hear anything, he says.

The road turns into the field and the truck comes to a stop, the children hop off into the grass. The wheatgrass is deep and swallows them up to the waist. Flies come buzzing out of the tomato crates. The sun has a red belly, the tomato field stretches far into the valley.

The agronomist is waiting by the crates, his tie flapping in front of his mouth. He bends over, inspects his pants and picks off the blades of wheatgrass. But the blades cling to his sleeves and back, they hike up his body faster than he can pick them off. Mother of all grass, he curses. He checks his watch, the dial burns in the sun and so does the wheatgrass. The blades shine with greed, the grass will stop at nothing to extend its reach. It even attaches itself to the wind. If it weren't in the field, it would be in the clouds, and the world would be smothered with wheatgrass.

The children pick up the crates, flies settle on the wart clusters. The flies are drunk from fermented tomatoes, they sparkle and they sting. The agronomist raises his head, closes his eyes and shouts, today's the last time I'm saying it, you're here to work, every day ripe tomatoes are left hanging and green ones are picked and red ones get trampled on the ground. A blade of wheatgrass dangles from the corner of his mouth, he tries to find it with his hand but can't, you're a disgrace to your school, he screams, you're doing more harm than good to our national agriculture. He locates the blade with the tip of his tongue and spits it out, fifteen crates a day, he says, that's the quota. You can't drink water all day, there's a half-hour break at twelve o'clock, that's when you can eat, drink, and go to the bathroom. A clump of thistle fluff is stuck in his hair.

The children set off into the field two by two, the empty crates swaying between them. The handles are slippery from squashed tomatoes, the plants themselves are poisonous green spotted with red. Even the smallest suckers. The wart clusters pick themselves bloody, the red tomatoes stupefy the children's eyes, the crates are deep and never full. Red juice oozes from the corners of the children's mouths, tomatoes fly around the heads and explode and color even the thistle clumps.

A girl sings:

I walked along a path above
And chanced upon a maid below

The girl puts a frog in her pocket, I'm taking it home with me, she says, covering her pocket with her hand. It will die, says Adina. The girl laughs, that doesn't matter, doesn't matter at all, she says. The agronomist looks up at the sky, catches a bit of thistle fluff with his hand and whistles the song about the maid. Two boys sit on a half-full crate, twins, nobody can tell them apart, they are two times one boy.

One twin sticks two thick red tomatoes under his shirt, the other fondles the tomato breasts with both hands, then crooks his fingers, squashes the tomatoes inside the shirt and looks with empty eyeballs at the girl with the frog. The shirt turns red, the girl with the frog laughs. The twin with the squashed tomatoes scratches the other in the face, they fall in a tangle onto the ground. Adina holds her hand out to help them up, but then pulls it back, which one started it, she asks. The girl with the frog shrugs her shoulders.

A necktie

With one hand the cyclist wheels his bike along the sidewalk, the gear chain rattles. His steps stay between the wheels as he walks past the park and toward the bridge.

The man with the reddish-blue flecked tie is coming off the bridge headed into the park. He holds a long white cigarette down by his knee, a wedding ring shines next to the filter. The man blows smoke into the shrubbery, and into the park which in the breath of fear causes people to lift their feet high. The man has a fingernail-sized birthmark between his ear and his collar.

The cyclist stops, pulls a cigarette from his pocket. He doesn't say a word, but the man with the tie raises his long white cigarette and gives the other a light. The cyclist spits out tobacco, the flame consumes a red ring on the tip of the cigarette. The cyclist blows smoke and walks on, wheeling his bicycle.

A branch cracks in the park. The cyclist turns his head, it's merely a blackbird in the shade that can only move by hopping. The cyclist draws in his cheeks and blows smoke into the park.

The man with the reddish-blue flecked tie stands at the crossing, waiting for the light. When it turns green he will hurry, because Clara has crossed the street.

Inside the store Clara stands next to the fur coats, the man's eyes watch her through the display window. He tosses his half-smoked cigarette onto the asphalt and blows a shred of smoke into the shop.

The man turns the tie rack. All the lamb fur coats are white except for one, which is green, as though the pasture had nibbled through the coat after it had been stitched together. The woman who buys it will certainly stand out in winter. She'll bring summer with her even in the middle of the snow.

The man with the reddish-blue flecked tie carries three ties to the window, the colors look different in this light, he says, which suits me the best. Clara holds a finger to her mouth, you or what you're wearing, she asks. Me, he says, as her hand squeezes the green lamb collar. None of them, she says, the one you have on is nicer. His shoes are polished, his chin is smooth, his hair has a part like a white thread, PAVEL, he says, reaching for her hand. Instead of shaking it he squeezes her fingers. She sees the seconds ticking on his watch, says her name, sees his thumbnail, then his ironed creases, he holds her hand too long under his thumb, LAWYER, he says. Behind the man is an empty shelf, dusty and full of fingerprints. You have a beautiful name, says Pavel, and a beautiful dress, that can't be from here. I got it from a Greek woman, says Clara.

Her eyes are empty and her tongue is hot, she can tell from the dust on the shelf that it's darker in the store and brighter on the street, that the midday hour is dividing the light between inside and out. She wants to go, but he is holding her hand. She feels a small shiny wheel spinning in her throat. He walks her through the door. And once outside, where his nose casts a slender shadow, she doesn't know whether the shiny wheel is her desire for the green lamb or for the man with the reddish-blue flecked tie. But she has the feeling that if the wheel in her throat is spinning for the green coat it's also catching on this man.

An old woman is sitting on the cathedral steps, she wears thick woolen stockings, a thick pleated coat and a white linen blouse. Beside her is a wicker basket covered with a damp cloth. Pavel lifts the cloth. Autumn crocuses, finger-thin bouquets, laid out in rows, each wound with white twine up to the flowers. Underneath, another cloth, more flowers, then another cloth, many layers of flowers and cloths and twine. Pavel picks out ten bouquets, one for each finger, he says, the old woman pulls a coin purse out of her blouse that's tied to a string. Clara sees the woman's nipples hanging on her skin like two screws. In Clara's hand the flowers smell of iron and grass. The same smell as the grass behind the wire factory after a rain.

When Pavel raises his head, the sidewalk drops out of the reflection in his sunglasses. On the streetcar tracks are the remnants of a run-over watermelon, sparrows pick at the red flesh. When the workers leave their food on the table, the sparrows eat the bread, says Clara, she can see his temples, and the trees moving away inside the glass lenses. He looks at her with the moving trees, brushes away a wasp, and talks. That's nice, he says to

Clara. What makes you say that, what's nice about working in a factory, says Clara.

Once inside the car Pavel ties his shoe while Clara sniffs at the crocuses. The car moves, the street is made of dust, a garbage bin is smoldering. A dog is lying on the road, Pavel honks, the dog gets up and slowly lies down in a patch of grass.

Clara is holding her keys, Pavel takes her hand and smells the crocus, she shows him which window is hers, I haven't seen your eyes, she says. He raises his fingers to his temple, she notices his wedding ring. He doesn't take off his sunglasses.

Summer entrails

There are no poplars on the plaza by the opera, so Opera Square isn't striped, only splotched by the shadows of pedestrians and passing streetcars. The yew trees keep their needles tightly bundled on top, sheltering the wood within against the sky and against the clock in the cathedral tower. Anyone who wants to sit down on the benches in front of the yews must first cross the hot asphalt. The needles on the lower branches in back of the benches have either fallen off or were never there, behind the benches the wood within the yews is open to the world.

Old men sit on the benches, seeking shade that will stay in one place. But the yew trees play tricks, they pretend the moving shadows of the streetcars are part of their shade. Then once the old men have sat down the yews let the streetcar shadows move on. The old men open their newspapers, the sun shines through their hands, and the miniature red roses planted by the benches glow through the newspaper into the dictator's forelock. The old men sit by themselves. They do not read.

Now and then a man who hasn't yet found an empty bench asks a friend who has, what are you doing, and the one sitting down fans his face with his newspaper, lays his hand on his knee and shrugs. You mean you're just sitting here thinking, asks the man standing. The other points to two empty milk bottles next to him and says, sitting, just sitting. That doesn't matter, says the man who's standing, doesn't matter at all. Then he shakes his head and walks on while the sitting man shakes his head and watches him leave.

Now and then lumber and planing tools pass through the minds of the old men and settle so close to the yew tree that the wooden tool handles can't be distinguished from the wood within the yew. Or from standing in line in the store where there wasn't enough milk and where the bread was counted.

Five white-gloved policemen stand on the plaza, their whistling throws the steps of the pedestrians out of sync. Nothing holds back the sun, and those who look up at the white balcony of the opera in the middle of the day feel their whole faces falling into the void. The policemen's whistles sparkle between their fingers. The whistles have deep, bulging bellies, it looks like each policeman is holding a large, handleless spoon. Their uniforms are dark blue, their faces young and pale. The heat swells the faces of the pedestrians, and they are so exposed in the sunlight they seem naked. The women cross the square carrying clear plastic bags with vegetables from the market. The men carry bottles. Anyone with empty hands, anyone not carrying fruit or vegetables or bottles, has eyes that rock back and forth and stare at the fruit and vegetables in the clear plastic bags as though they were the entrails of summer. Tomatoes, onions, apples under the women's ribs. Bottles under the ribs of the men. And the white balcony in the middle of it all. And eyes that are empty.

The square has been cordoned off, the streetcars are stopped behind the yew trees. Funeral music creeps through the narrow streets behind the plaza, where it leaves its echo, and the sky stretches above the city. The women and men set down their see-through bags in front of their shoes. A truck comes out of one of the narrow streets and slowly crosses the plaza. Its side panels are down and draped with red flag cloth, the policemen's whistles fall silent, white cuffs glow on the sleeves of the driver.

The truck is carrying an open coffin.

The dead man's hair is white, his face fallen in, his mouth deeper than his eye sockets. Fronds of green fern quiver around his chin.

A man takes a brandy bottle out of his plastic bag. As he drinks one eye is focused on the brandy trickling into his mouth and the other on the dead man's uniform. When I was in the military, a lieutenant told me that dead officers become monuments, he says. The woman next to him takes an apple out of her bag. As she bites, one eye is focused on the dead man's face and the other on his huge portrait being carried behind the coffin. The face on the picture is twenty years younger than the face in the coffin, she says. The man sets his bottle down in front of his shoes and says, a man who's mourned a lot when he dies becomes a tree, and a man who isn't mourned at all becomes a stone. But what if somebody dies in one place, says the woman, and the people doing the mourning are somewhere else, then it doesn't do any good, the person still becomes a stone.

Following the dead man's portrait is a red velvet cushion with the dead man's medals, and after the medals comes a withered woman on the arm of a young man. And bringing up the whole procession is a military band. The brass instruments gleam, enlarged by the light. Behind the brass band come the mourners, shuffling their feet, the women carry gladioli wrapped in cellophane, the children carry white fringed asters.

Walking among the mourners is Pavel.

Sitting at the edge of the plaza, where the man drank his brandy, is an empty bottle, and next to that a half-eaten apple. The funeral music hums quietly through the cramped, crooked streets. The Heroes' Cemetery is outside the town center. The square is littered with trampled gladioli, the streetcars lurch into motion.

The old men walk across the deserted plaza, their empty milk bottles rattle. They stop for no reason. Above them the white balcony of the opera has moved its columns into the shadow of the wall. The holes in the soft asphalt below are from the high heels of the women mourners.

Days of melons, days of pumpkins

Waterlogged cotton wool is lying in the toilet bowl, the water is rusty, having sucked the blood from the cotton. Melon seeds are lying on the seat.

When the women wear cotton wool between their thighs, they carry the blood of melons in their bellies. Every month come the days of the melons and the weight of the melons, it hurts.

With melon blood any woman can bind any man she wants, said Clara. The women in the wire factory talk about how it's done: once a month late in the afternoon they stir a little melon blood into the man's tomato soup. On that day they don't put the tureen on the table, they fill each bowl at the stove. The melon blood is in a ladle next to the oven, waiting for the man's soup bowl. They stir the soup with the ladle until the blood is dissolved.

During the days of the melons the wire mesh passes in front of their faces before clambering onto the large spool where it is measured by the meter. The looms bang away, the women's hands are rusty, their eyes dull.

The women from the factory bind the men to themselves in the late afternoon or evening, said Clara, in the morning they don't have enough time. In the morning they hurry off from the men's sleep, and carry a bed full of sleep and a room full of sticky air with them into the factory.

But according to the servant's daughter it's best to bind the men in the morning, on an empty stomach. During the days of the melons the officer's wife slips four dashes of melon blood into the officer's morning coffee, before he goes off to his casino. She brings him his coffee in the same cup as always, without any sugar. She knows he'll take two spoons of sugar and stir it into the coffee for a long time. The blood bits dissolve faster than the sugar. The best is the blood from the second day, the officer's wife told the servant's daughter. The wife's melon blood is in every step the officer takes on the bridge, every day he spends drinking in the casino. Each bit of blood lasts a week, four bits cover the whole month.

Each blood bit has to be as big as the thumbnail of the man the woman wants to bind, said the officer's wife. The melon blood dissolves in the coffee and clots again after it's run down his throat, she said. It doesn't go past his heart, it doesn't trickle into his stomach. The melon blood cannot contain the officer's desire, there's no remedy for that because his desire refuses to be bound. His desire flies to other women, but the melon blood winds around his heart. It clots and locks the heart in. The officer's heart is closed to the image of other women, said the servant's daughter, he can betray his wife but he cannot abandon her.

Someone has written on the wall of the toilet stall:

'Tis eve on the hillside
The bagpipes are distantly wailing

Two lines from a famous poem the children learn in school. The servant's daughter claimed to recognize the handwriting. It's the physics teacher, she said, I can tell from the way he writes the d and the l. The lines run at an angle up the wall.

Adina feels a warm rush between her thighs, then hears someone latching the door to the neighboring stall. She pushes her elbows against her thighs, she wants to keep the rushing smooth and even. But her belly doesn't know what smooth and even is. Over the toilet tank is a small window with spiderwebs instead of a pane. It never has a spider, the noise of the tank drives it away. Every day, a band of light perches on the wall and watches everything including how the women rub newsprint between their hands until the writing is grainy and the fingers gray. Rubbed newsprint doesn't scratch the thighs.

At the faculty meeting the cleaning woman announced there was no toilet paper for the teachers' toilet. For three days in a row, she said, I set out a new roll, but each roll was stolen within fifteen minutes on each of the three days, so now three rolls have to last for three weeks.

Well, corncobs and beet leaves were good enough for you in the bourgeois-aristocratic regime, the director said. Back then the only people who had newsprint were the estate owners. Now everyone has a newspaper at home. But all of a sudden newsprint's too rough for such sophisticated gentlemen and ladies.

The director tore off a corner of newspaper the size of his palm, rubbed the piece between his hands, it's as easy as washing your hands, he said, nobody can tell me he doesn't know how to wash his hands. Anyone who hasn't mastered that by the age of thirty really ought to learn how. His eyebrows drew together above his nose, thin and gray, like a mouse's tail on his forehead.

The cleaning lady wiggled on her chair and smiled. She stood up and the director looked down at the floor. It's true that these days everyone has a newspaper at home, but Comrade Director you must have forgotten that beet leaves were too soft, the fingers used to tear right through, she said. Ivy leaves were better. That's enough, said the director, or there'll be no end to it.

The servant's daughter tapped Adina with her foot, the cleaning lady can get away with anything, she said, the director's sleeping with her. Her husband's an electrician, yesterday he came to school and spat on the director's table and tore two buttons off his suit. The buttons rolled under the wardrobe. After the electrician had gone, the director interrupted the physics teacher in the middle of class and made him move the wardrobe away from the wall and then go to the tailor's for needle and thread. But he wasn't allowed to take the suit. The director said, the cleaning lady has to sew those buttons back on herself.

The cleaning lady is only allowed to cut up the last pages of the paper—news reports, the sports section and the TV programs. She has to give the first pages with the party news and the pictures of the dictator to the director, they're for the collection of the party secretary.

Adina flushes the toilet. In front of the bathroom mirror her hair is threaded with light, she turns the faucet. The door to the neighboring stall is unlatched and out steps the director. He stands next to Adina in the mirror. He opens his mouth, I think I have a toothache, he says to the mirror. Yes Mr. Director, she says, his molars have gold fillings, COMRADE DIRECTOR, he says, his molars glistening a yellowish orange, like a pumpkin. The days of the melons are for men days of pumpkins, thinks Adina. The director takes his creased and pointed handkerchief and wipes his mouth. Come to my office after your last class, he says, plucking a hair from Adina's shoulder. Yes, Comrade Director, she says.

The forelock shines above the blackboard, and the black of the eye shines, catching the strand of light that falls through the window. The children move their elbows as they write, the composition is called THE TOMATO HARVEST. Adina stands by the window next to the string of light. Inside the notebooks the tomato field is growing once again, made of warts and letters.

The girl with the frog reads:

> For two weeks the pupils of our school have been helping the farmers in the agriculture. Our class is helping with the tomato harvest. It is beautiful to work in the fields of our fatherland. It is helpful and healthy.

In front of the school is a square of yellow grass, beyond the square are housing blocks, and in between the housing blocks is one freestanding house. Adina looks at the houseleeks growing on the roof. The housing blocks have pushed the garden up against the wall. The grapevines wrap around the window and stop it from moving.

In the morning, when I get up, reads the girl with the frog, I put on my work clothes instead of my uniform. I don't take any notebooks or books, just a bottle of water, a butter sandwich, and an apple.

One of the twins shouts BUTTER and drums on his seat with his fists.

A horse cart stops in front of the lone house with the houseleeks, a man climbs down and carries a mesh bag full of bread loaves through the garden into the house. He keeps close to the wall, behind the grapevines.

At eight o'clock all the pupils gather in front of the school, reads the girl with the frog. A man drives us out to the field on a truck. There's lots of laughing on the way. Every morning the agronomist waits at the edge of the field. He is tall and thin. He wears a suit and has nice clean hands. He is a friendly man.

Except yesterday he slapped you, says the twin. Why didn't you write that, says Adina. The horse in front of the empty cart is standing completely still.

The other twin lowers his head below his desk, you can't write about the slapping, he says. He takes the slice of bread smeared with lard that he's holding and sticks it on the composition.

The girl with the frog tears a white ribbon out of her braid, sticks the end of her braid in her mouth and cries.

The man carries an empty mesh bag back past the grapevines and climbs onto the cart. A dwarf crosses the grass in front of the school. His red shirt glows, he is carrying a watermelon.

Comrade, says the girl with the frog to Adina.

A clock is set on the wall over the door to the director's office, its hands measure the coming and going of the pupils and teachers. Over the head of the director is the forelock and the black inside the eye. The rug has an ink stain, a display case holds the speeches of the dictator. The director smells of bitter tobacco perfume, you know why I've called you here, he says. Next to his elbow is a dahlia that faces away from the desk, the water in the vase is cloudy. No, says Adina, I don't know. His eyebrows draw together gray and thin, you told the pupils they should eat as many tomatoes as they can because they're not allowed to take any home. And you also said something about exploiting minors. A fleck of dust lingers in the light above the dahlia. That's not true, Comrade Director, says Adina. Her voice is quiet, the director steps across the ink stain and stands behind Adina's chair. His breath is dry and short, he slides his hand into her blouse and moves down her back. Don't say COMRADE, he says, now's not the time for that.

Adina's back stays rigid, her disgust doesn't let it bend, her mouth says, my back is fine, no warts there. The director laughs, very well, he says. She presses her back against the chair, he removes his hand, I won't report it this time, he says. He brushes against the dahlia. And who will believe you, says Adina. She sees the blood of the melons in the reddish leaves of the dahlia. I'm not like that, he says. His sweat smells heavier than the tobacco in the perfume. He combs his hair.

His comb has blue teeth.

The cat and the dwarf

A line of heads passes between the rusty spools of wire in the factory yard. The man at the gatehouse looks up into the sky. What he sees is the loudspeaker next to the gate.

In the morning, between six and seven-thirty, music comes out of this loudspeaker. The gateman calls it morning music. He uses it as a clock. Anyone who passes through the gate after the music has stopped is late to work. Anyone who isn't stepping to the music on his way to the lathes and looms, anyone crossing through the yard when it is quiet is written up and reported.

The marching songs are loud even before it's light outside. The wind beats against the corrugated tin roof. The rain pounds on the asphalt. The women's stockings are spattered, the men's hat brims turn to gutters. Out on the street the daylight comes sooner, but inside the factory the wire spools are still black and wet from the night. Even in summer it takes the day longer to reach the factory yard than to light the street outside.

The gateman chews sunflower seeds and spits the shells into the afternoon. They land on the ground, on the threshold. The woman who shares the gatehouse duty sits beside him, knitting. She wears a green smock. She has a gap in the middle of her teeth. She counts the spools of wire and wire mesh out loud, through the gap in her teeth. A striped cat is sprawled at her feet.

The phone rings in the gatehouse. The gateman hears it ring and listens with his temples, without turning his head. He keeps his eyes on the people passing through the spools of wire. The gatewoman lifts her knitting needle to the gap between her teeth, then sticks it down her smock and scratches between her breasts. The cat twitches her ears and watches. The cat's eyes are golden grapes. The spool tally gets caught in the gap between the woman's teeth and inside the eyes of the cat. The telephone is shrill. The ringing catches on the wool, the yarn climbs into the gatewoman's hand. The ringing climbs into the cat's stomach. The cat climbs over the gateman's shoe and runs into the factory yard. The gateman doesn't answer the phone.

When she's inside the factory yard, the cat is all rust and wire mesh. On top of the factory roof she is all corrugated tin, and outside the offices she is all asphalt. By the washroom, sand. And in the workrooms the cat is all shafts and cogs and oil.

The gateman can see heads emerging among the spools. Sparrows come flitting out of the wire. The gateman glances up at the sky. A single sparrow flying in the sun is something light, only a flock is heavy. The corrugated tin slices the afternoon at an angle. The twittering of the sparrows is hoarse.

The heads come nearer, on their way out of the factory, leaving the wire behind. The gateman can already make out their necks. He paces up and down. He yawns, his tongue is thick, it squeezes his eyes shut during the empty time when the sun sends streaks of moisture down his chin. When the gateman stands in the sunlight, a bald spot appears, sleeping under strands of hair. The gateman still doesn't see the hands and bags of the passing heads.

For the gateman, yawning is waiting. When the workers leave the wire, their bags become his bags. The bags are searched. The bags are light, and swing from the hands holding them. Unless there's iron stashed inside, in which case they hang stiffly. The gateman notices that. The women's purses also hang stiffly if they are carrying something made of iron. Anything that can be stolen from the factory is made of iron.

The gateman's hands don't rummage through every bag, they simply know which to search when the faces pass by, because there is a change in the air. A change he can sense in his face, somewhere between his nose and his mouth. The gateman lets himself be inhaled by this air, lets his intuition decide between one bag and another.

His decision also depends on the gatehouse shade, and on the taste of the sunflower seeds in his mouth. If a few kernels are rancid his tongue turns bitter. His cheekbones clench up, his eyes grow stubborn. His fingertips tremble. But after the first bag his fingers gain confidence. His palm presses against the foreign objects, his grabbing becomes greedy. Rummaging through a bag is for him the same thing as grabbing a face. He can cause the faces to go from chalk to blush. And they don't recover. When he waves them on, the faces leaving the gate are either caved in or swollen up. And they stay distraught long after they've left. Their vision and hearing stay blurred, so that the sun seems like a giant version of the gateman's hand. And their noses are no longer enough, they have to gasp for air in the streetcar, with mouths and eyes in faces that are no longer their own.

As he searches, the gateman hears their empty swallowing. Throats turn dry as a vise, fear rummages through stomachs, and passes out of their bowels as foul air that lingers at knee height. The gatekeeper can smell the fear. And if he spends longer searching a particular bag, many are so afraid they pass not one, but two quiet farts.

The gatewoman once told Clara that the gateman is a strict believer. That explains why he doesn't love people, she said. He punishes those who don't believe. And he admires those who do. He doesn't love the believers, but he does respect them. He respects the party secretary because the party secretary believes in the party. He respects the director because the director believes in power.

The gatewoman pulled a bobby pin out of her hair, stuck it in the gap between her teeth and rewound her bun. Most people who believe in something, said Clara, are high party officials, and they have no need for the gateman or his respect.

The gatewoman plunged her pin deep into her hair and said, but there are other believers too. Clara was standing in the door, the other woman was sitting in the gatehouse. Do you believe in God, she asked Clara. Clara peered into the bun on top of the woman's head and focused on the bend of the bobby pin, which was made of wire. The tines had disappeared so only the bend was visible, and it was as thin as a single strand of hair. Only brighter. Sometimes I believe and sometimes I don't, Clara told the gatewoman, and if nothing's troubling me, then I forget.

The gatewoman dusted off the phone with the corner of a curtain and said, the gatekeeper says some people simply aren't capable of believing. While she spoke she saw her face in the window-pane and her smock, which looked darker in the glass. The gateman says that the workers don't believe in their jobs and they don't believe in God, for them He's just a day off work. And maybe, if God's willing, a roasted chicken for Sunday dinner, stuffed with its own liver. The gateman doesn't eat poultry, said the gatewoman.

The flock of sparrows scatters. The windows in the factory halls are broken, the sparrows find the holes in the glass, and fly into the main workroom faster than the gateman can see. The gate-woman laughs and says, don't even bother to look or they'll fly right through your forehead. The gateman stares at his hands, at the black hairs on his fingers, at his wrists. The shadow of the afternoon slices his pants below his knees. The dust beside the spools of wire spins around itself.

A knife, a smeared canning jar, a newspaper, a crust of bread. And under the paper a handful of screws. Well well, says the gateman. The man closes his bag.

A letter, a bottle of nail polish. A plastic bag and a book. A jacket stuffed in a shopping bag. A lipstick drops out of the jacket pocket. The gateman bends over. He opens the lipstick, rubs a red stripe on his wrist. He licks the stripe off with his tongue, pfui he says, rotten raspberries and mosquitoes.

The man has a wound on his thumb. The buckles on his bag are rusty. The gateman opens the bag and takes out first a folding ruler, then a cap, and from under the cap a clothes iron. Look at that, says the gateman. All I did was repair the plug, says the man. On factory time, says the gateman. He sets the iron in the gatehouse and curses, mother of all plugs. The gatewoman places the iron on her hand and, stretching her fingers, irons her palm flat.

A purse. A clump of cotton wool drops onto the ground. The man with the wounded thumb bends over to pick it up. The woman pulls a strand of hair behind her ear, she takes the cotton wool out of the hand with the wounded thumb. A sunflower seed and an ant are clinging to the cotton.

The sun flashes white on Clara's teeth as she laughs, and the gap between the gatewoman's teeth laughs, and the gateman sends Clara through.

The man with the wounded thumb takes his cap out of his bag and spins it on his forefinger like a wheel. The gatewoman laughs, the gap between her teeth is a megaphone that makes her laughter echo. The man with the wounded thumb peers into the spinning circles of his cap and sings:

The money came the money went
We owe the landlord two months' rent

His fist is a wheel, a vein in the crook of his arm pulses thick and thin. His eyes are following the gatewoman's knitting needles.

He's thrown us out now on the street
Yes life is always such a treat.

His mouth sings, his eyes are narrow and his fist is whirling. And his other hand, the empty one with the wounded thumb, does not move to close the rusty buckles on his bag. The man's song is a song of waiting to get the iron back.

An acacia leaf flutters by the crack of the door, then races off and flies and flies. The gatewoman watches it go. The leaf is yellow like the eyes of the cat. The man with the wounded thumb looks at the clock.

Every year the cat has kittens. They're tiger-striped just like she is. She eats them right away, while they're still slippery wet and blind. The cat mourns for a week after devouring her young. She ranges through the factory yard. Her belly is flat, her stripes narrow, there's nothing she can't move through or past.

As long as the cat's in mourning she does not eat meat. Only young grass tips and the salty residue that collects on the stairs in the back courtyard.

The women on the mesh looms claim that the cat came from the outskirts of town. And the warehouse supervisor says she emerged from the factory yard, from the boxes of iron shavings, where the rain barely leaks through. He says she was wet and rusty and no bigger than an apple when he found her there on his way from the warehouse to the offices. And that the kitten's eyes were shut. The supervisor set the kitten on a leather glove and carried it to the gateman, who placed it in a fur cap.

And I fed that thing milk through a straw for thirty days, says the gatewoman. And raised her myself since nobody wanted her. After a week, says the gateman, the kitten was able to open its eyes. And I was shocked to see the image of the supervisor deep inside those eyes. And to this day, whenever the cat purrs, he says, the supervisor is right there in both of her eyes.

As far as the cat is concerned, the factory is as big as her nose. She sniffs everything and everywhere. She sniffs in the workrooms, in the remotest corners, where people sweat and freeze and shout and cry and steal. She sniffs up and down the gaps between the spools, where the grass is choked out and where people squish and pant and make love standing up. Where copulating is as greedy and hidden as stealing.

At the rear entrance to the factory, which is reserved for trucks, the roof is made of tar paper, the gutter of split tires, and the fence is an assemblage of dented car doors and willow whips. Beyond this entrance is a crooked street called VICTORY STREET. The gutter lets the rain out onto Victory Street. Next to the rear entrance is the warehouse containing mountains of protective clothing—gray padded jackets, green leather aprons and gloves, and gray rubber boots. The warehouse has a small window overlooking the street. And inside, below the window, is a large overturned crate that serves as a table, and a small overturned crate that serves as a chair. On the table is a list with the names of all the workers. And on the chair sits the warehouse supervisor, Grigore.

Grigore sells gold, says the gatewoman, gold necklaces. And wedding rings. He buys them from an old Gypsy who lost a leg in the war. That man lives on the edge of town, near the Heroes'

Cemetery. The Gypsy buys the gold from a young Serbian, who lives in a village in the corner of the country where Romania and Hungary and Serbia all meet. He has relatives in Serbia and travels there frequently as part of the local border traffic. He also has a brother-in-law who works as a customs official at the border.

Now and then Grigore acquires merchandise from Russia as well. The thick gold necklaces come from Russia and the thin ones from Serbia. The thick ones are made of die-cut hearts and the thin ones of die-cut dice. The wedding rings come from Hungary.

When Grigore closes one hand and slowly opens his fingers, the chains slither out like golden wire. He lets the ends dangle and holds them up to the light from the small window.

For a woman working at the factory, six months of rusty wire have to pass through her hands before she takes her wages to Grigore and a gold chain is draped around her neck. But then a few days afterward, late in the evening, just when bare feet are stepping on a rug and the gold is glittering above a nightgown, there comes a knock at the door and two men are standing there, one in a suit and another in uniform. The light in the hall is dim but enough to see a rubber truncheon dangling alongside the leg of the uniform. The man in the suit speaks in curt sentences, his cheek is smooth and shiny, a spot of light rises and falls. The voice stays quiet, almost flat, cold. The man's shoes stand on the edge of the rug. The chain is confiscated from the neck.

Grigore recovers it the following morning, when the first streetcar is nearly empty and the lights are blinking off and on from all the jolting. The man in the suit climbs in at the stop by the brewery and silently hands him a matchbox.

On those days Grigore is the first person at the factory, he arrives when the water is still lazy under the bridge and the sky still hunched over with darkness. He's cold and lights a cigarette. The loudspeaker is mute as he passes among the spools, trailing the smoke from his cigarette, carrying his gold chains. A few hours later he again lets them dangle and run through his fingers in front of the small window overlooking Victory Street. And the money reappears, the same but different, just like the same but different images that reappear in the eyes of the cat.

The gateman says that in the evening Grigore regularly goes to the police and reports whom he sold gold chains to in the morning. But he does not report the wedding rings.

The gateman respects Grigore the warehouse supervisor, because Grigore believes in his money.

Well the black market is exactly that, says the gatewoman, after all no one's making them buy anything. And black business is risky business. The gateman says, one person has, the other needs, and so the world turns. Everyone does what he can.

The cat can also smell whenever the supervisor takes a woman off to the left corner of the warehouse. He leads them down an aisle between the heaps of clothing and up to a lair hollowed out of the gray mountain, right below the window. The women lie on the slope of clothing, so when they lift their legs their feet are the same height as their head. When Grigore undoes his pants, the cat comes in off the roof and sits on the top of the mountain, overlooking the lair. From the women's point of view the cat is sitting upside down, because their rubber boots are raised above their eyes. The eyes of the women race through their foreheads to the eyes of the cat. Shoo her away from there, say the women, shoo her away. And Grigore says, that doesn't matter, she can't see anything, let her be, that doesn't matter at all. The cat twitches her eyes and watches.

Afterward the women stand in front of the desk, covered in sweat, with a gray padded jacket over their arm. They find their name on the supervisor's list and sign for their clothing. The cat doesn't wait for them to sign. She clambers outside and saunters between the wire spools in the courtyard and into the workrooms.

The image remains fixed for a while in the eyes of the cat, so everyone can see what's happened. And everyone talks about it, about the latest love hastily performed standing up or lying down. The talk about the love is also hasty. They all rest their hands on the wire, wherever their fingers happen to be when the cat comes near. Because no image grows very old. Because another one comes along and is fixed for a while in the eyes of the cat. And envy spurs each woman on, as does the oil splattered on her face, convincing her that she will be next, that the next image in the eyes of the cat will feature her. Come spring or come fall, when the padded jacket wears out and tears at the elbows and when the wind scratches cold or warm against the tar paper and blows through the fence onto Victory Street, the other women will be watching. Because the cat will carry their thighs through the factory, naked in the lair and spread wide and raised higher than their heads—the thighs now resting under their smocks in front of their looms.

When the cat mourns her young, her eyes have no image, but that's only one week during the year. Whoever is seized by love in the haste of this fleeting blind week is lucky, say the women. They believe no one will see them because there will be no image in the eyes of the cat.

Many bribe the gatewoman to tell them when this week will be. They all do, she says, so I fill the calendar, and I tell each of them whatever I want.

And each woman tries to jump the queue, rushing into the false week of mourning with short hasty thrusts.

But during the actual week of mourning, the love lines all get tangled, between the workrooms and the factory yard, the washroom and office, and so the coupling men and women do end up being seen, by the gatekeeper, the cleaning woman, the foreman and the stoker. There is one small difference, though: because there are no images in the eyes of the cat during the real week of mourning, each of these encounters remains a rumor.

The women's children all look like Grigore, says the gatewoman. Thank god the mothers don't bring them to the factory. I've never seen the children all grouped together, only one here and one there. Short or tall, skinny or fat, black-haired or blond. Girls and boys. When they stand next to each other you can tell they're siblings. They're all different, says the gatewoman, but every one of their faces has a palm-sized piece of Grigore.

From the moment they're born, the women's children suffer from sleeplessness. The doctors say it comes from the machine oil.

These children start growing and for a few years it seems they will grow up and away from the factory.

But sooner or later, says the gatewoman, they come here to the gatehouse looking for their mothers. It's rarely anything urgent. Most of the time there's no reason.

The gatewoman says the children stand there next to the gatehouse and tell her their names so the gateman can call their mothers. And that while they're standing there they clutch their cheeks with their fingertips because they're afraid. That they don't see either of the gatekeepers. That from the moment they say their names they only have eyes for the wire, the spools, the sunken factory yard, which they stare at with empty eyes. And that the longer they stand there, the more the palm-sized piece of Grigore starts to show in their faces.

And the gatewoman sees the rust on their small or large shirts, on their small or large clothes, on their knee socks. While the children are standing and waiting next to the gatehouse, some small, some bigger, some nearly grown-up, the gatewoman can always spot the rusty stains—every child has one on some piece of clothing, like a toothed and tattered leaf.

The rust comes from the hands of the mothers, from the same hands that mix melon blood into the men's soup before dinner. The black rims on their fingernails dissolve when they do the laundry. And then the rust is not in the water and not in the foam. It's in the fabric. And there's nothing to do about that: drying in the wind doesn't help, or ironing, or stain removers, says the gatewoman.

Even ten years later the gatewoman recognizes Grigore's many children who have no idea they are related. By then tons of rust and wire mesh have been driven through the gate. And new tons of rust and wire mesh have been woven and piled in the same spot, before the grass can find any sun to grow. And by then these children, too, are working in the factory. They never wished it, they're here only because the factory is all they know. From the tip of their noses to the tips of their toes they never find another way because there is no other way for them to find. Nothing but this gutter of poverty, hopelessness and tedium, from mother to child and on to that child's children. One day without warning they discover they have no choice: at first they're angry and loud, then eventually they become soft and quiet, puttering from one day to the next. The tang of the machine oil still stings their nostrils, their hands are long since rimmed with black. They get married and thrust their shrunken love into each other's bellies during the break between day shift and night shift. And they get children. Who lie in rusty diapers. These children grow and put on small and then large shirts, clothes, socks and stockings. They stand right next to the gatehouse with their tattered leaves of rust. And wait. And they don't know that they'll never find a way, that nothing else will occur to them.

Grigore's mother also worked in the factory. As did the mother of the gatewoman.

The knitting needles are resting on the table. The factory yard is quiet. The wind smells of malt. Just past the rooftops is the brewery cooling tower. And jutting out of the tower is a large insulated pipe that stretches over the street and into the river. Steam comes out of the pipe. During the day the steam gets shredded by the passing streetcars. During the night it is a white curtain. Some people say the steam smells of rats, because inside the iron vats, which are bigger than the gatehouse, the river rats get drunk and drown in the beer.

On the eighth day, says the gatekeeper, God had a clump of hair left over from Adam and Eve. He used that to make the feathered creatures. And on the ninth day God faced the great void and belched. And from that belch He created beer.

The gatehouse shadow has widened. The sun is looking for the shortest path between Victory Street and the wire spools in the yard. The sun is boxy and squeezed in at the edges, with a gray spot right in the middle.

There are days in late summer when the loudspeaker up by the gatehouse crackles. Then the gateman stares at the sky for a long time and says, up there, above those tin roofs, over the city, higher than the brewery cooling tower, the sun's turned into a rusty water tap.

Outside the gate is a pothole where the sparrows powder themselves in the dust. Lying on the ground between them is a screw.

The gatekeepers sit in the gatehouse. They play cards. The iron is resting on the edge of the table. The gatekeeper confiscated the iron and reported the man with the wounded thumb to the administration. Tomorrow the man with the wounded thumb will receive a written reprimand.

Sparrows are hopping inside the workroom. Their feet and beaks are black from the machine oil. They peck at sunflower seeds and melon seeds and bread crumbs. When the workroom is empty the letters on the slogans are larger than ever, WORK and HONOR and PARTY, and the lamp by the door to the dressing room has a long neck. The dwarf with the red shirt and the tall shoes sweeps the oily floor with an oily broom. Sitting on a nearby loom is a watermelon. It is bigger than his head. The watermelon has light and dark stripes.

The light slants through the door to the factory yard. And the cat sits next to the door and chews on a piece of bacon rind. The dwarf looks through the door into the yard.

And the dust flies without a reason. And the door creaks.

Nuts

The woman with the gnarled hands spits on the cloth and rubs the apples until they shine. She sets out the shining apples in a row, red cheeks in front, scars toward the back. The apples are small and malformed. The scale is empty. To weigh the fruit she uses two iron bird head weights, their beaks swing past each other until weights and apples balance out and come to a stop. Then the old woman counts out loud until her eyes come as close together as the iron beaks. Like the beaks her eyes are hard and silent because they know the price.

All the vendors in the market hall are old. Within the concrete walls, under the concrete roof, behind the concrete tables and on the concrete floor the country village can be seen in their faces—gardens fending off the creeping wheatgrass.

Liviu has been talking about these villages ever since he took a job teaching in the part of the country cut off by the Danube.

He talks about summer days that grow tired until they snap shut between the eyes, days that amount to nothing more than the evening, when the head sags into sleep before the body can come to rest. He tells about the wakeful sleep of the young and the leaden sleep of the old. And about how in their nighttime wakefulness and leaden sleep the day's toil keeps on trembling in their fingers and trudging in their feet. And how their ears mistake their own snoring for the voice of the village policeman and the mayor, who tell them even in their dreams what must be planted in every garden, every flower bed. Because the policeman and the mayor have their lists and their accounting. And they expect their tribute, no matter if flea beetles, worms, snails or mildew come and devour everything or not. Even if rain forgets the village and the sun burns it down to the last fiber and flattens it so night climbs in from all sides at once.

Liviu visits the city three times a year. He doesn't feel at home in Paul's apartment, where he lived for some time, or in the city where he lived for a long time. In the morning he asks for brandy and calls it PLUM MILK.

When Liviu visits, Paul says that he moves like a trapped dog inside the apartment and like a runaway dog when he's out in town. And that Liviu is hanging by a thread, and that this thread is about to snap, and that Liviu knows it and so he talks and talks until his voice is hoarse.

Liviu tells Paul and Adina about the nights in his village, where only two corners are lit—at the houses of the mayor and the policeman. Two yards, two sets of steps, two gardens where even the foliage is guarded by light. Singled out and quiet.

Everything else is buried in darkness. The dogs run off into the night and bark only in places where the bulbs have long burned out, where the trees lead the houses toward the Danube as they lean out over the water.

You can't see the water, says Liviu, and you don't hear it in the village. You only hear it in the middle of your head, but the pressure's so strong you can't feel your feet. As though you could drown right there on dry ground, he says, right inside your own ears.

Every now and then you hear shots in the distance, Liviu explains. No louder than a cracking branch. Only different, very different. When that happens the dogs go quiet for a moment and then start barking even louder. That means someone was trying to swim upriver during the night and cross the Danube where it forms the border. On his own. When you hear that sound you know it's all over. He stares at the edge of the table, presses one hand against the back of the chair and closes his eyes for a moment. So I drink, says Liviu. The plum milk burns, my eyes jitter so the lightbulb starts to float, or the candle when there's no electricity. I keep drinking until I forget the shots, says Liviu. Until the plum milk makes my legs go wavy. And I keep forgetting, he says, until there's nothing more to think about, until there's absolutely no escaping the fact that the Danube has cut off the village from the rest of the world.

Out in the country you're a boy from the city, and here in town you're a peasant, says Paul. You ought to come back. The city knows who we are, you and I, out there you have thousands of village policemen guarding just a few hundred strips of asphalt.

Paul starts singing and Liviu hums along:

Face without face
Forehead of sand
Voice without voice
What could I trade with you
One call a brother
For a single cigarette

Liviu climbs onto the chair and swats the hanging lampshade with his hand. The cord swings back and forth. Along with its shadow.

My only thought is this
What could I sell to you
My coat is old and rumpled
With just one button left

Paul's eyes are half closed and Liviu's have swum out of his head with all the singing. But maybe they aren't his eyes at all—perhaps it's just his mouth that's so wet.

Night comes and sews a sack
Sews a sack of darkness

Liviu catches the lampshade with his hand. He stops singing, and Paul bangs more loudly on the table.

Stepmothergrass has bitter blades
The freight train whistles at the station
Little child where are your parents
Sitting on the asphalt is a barefoot shoe

Paul looks out the window at the antennas of the neighboring apartment block. He stands up and shoves his chair to the table. Then he glances up at Liviu, who laughs without making a sound. Too bad lamp cords don't just hang down from the sky, Liviu says into the silence, because then anyone could go outside and hang himself wherever he wanted.

Don't look at me like that, Liviu says to Paul. The sentence drops right into Paul's face. Paul leaves the room, Liviu climbs off the chair. When he's back on the floor he says to Adina as well as to himself, if you ask me Paul isn't much of a doctor.

Paul sits alone in the kitchen, talking to himself but loud enough so the others can hear. Tonight, he says, a couple came to the hospital. The man had a small hatchet stuck in his head. The handle was on top and looked like it was growing out of his hair. There wasn't a drop of blood to be seen. The doctors gathered around the man. The woman said it happened a week ago. The man laughed and said he felt good. One female doctor said all we can do is cut off the handle, the blade can't be removed because the brain has gotten used to it. The doctors went ahead and removed the blade. And the man died.

Adina and Liviu briefly exchange glances.

The carrots on the table are wooden, the onions stunted. The tinsmith is standing behind a pile of nuts. But he isn't wearing his leather apron and there isn't any string around his neck, his wedding ring is on his finger. He sticks his hand into the nuts, they rattle like gravel. Neither hand is missing a finger. The man with the nuts is not the tinsmith with the fruit in the newspaper cones. The man with the nuts doesn't say, eat slowly so you can savor every bite for a long time.

But he could be.

The man has the tinsmith's eyes, he looks at the scale, the bird head weights go up and down. The beaks come to a stop and the eyes know the price. Adina opens her bag, the nuts tumble inside. Two fall to the ground. Adina bends over.

A man with a reddish-blue flecked tie beats her to it. Adina bumps against his shoulder, he's already picked up the nuts that rolled away. Adina notices a birthmark on his neck, as big as the tip of her finger. The man tosses both nuts into her bag, evidently they didn't want to stay with you, he says, you know there's a reason people say DUMB NUT, can I have one. She nods. He reaches into her bag and takes two. He closes his hand and squeezes one against the other as he walks alongside her. The shell cracks, he opens his hand. One nut is whole, the other broken. Adina looks at the white brain in his palm. The man drops pieces of shell onto the ground and eats the nutmeat. His birthmark hops, his forehead glistens, he sticks the other nut in his jacket pocket. What's your name, he asks. A milky residue is on his teeth, the nuts rattle in her bag with every step. Adina clutches the bag under her arm, what does that have to do with nuts, she says. What are we going to do now, he says. Nothing, says Adina.

She turns and walks away from him.

Pavel stands by the left side entrance to the market hall and watches Adina leave, the light twists strings of dust before his eyes. His cheeks move, his tongue uncovers chewed bits of nut lodged between his teeth, his birthmark has stopped hopping. He takes the remaining nut out of his pocket and lays it on the asphalt. He places the edge of his heel right over the shell. Then he steps on the nut with all his weight. And the shell cracks. Pavel bends over, picks the brain out of the shell, then chews and swallows.

Parked outside the right entrance to the market hall is a black car with a yellow license plate. The number on the plate is low—a number of privilege. The man in the car is resting his head on the steering wheel and staring absently into the market hall. He watches an old woman. The concrete table cuts her stomach off from her legs. The old woman is sifting red paprika, which trickles out of the sieve like red spiderwebs, always landing in the same place. The mountain under the sieve grows quickly.

The young lady isn't exactly approachable, says Pavel. Doesn't matter, says the man in the car, that doesn't matter. The old woman knocks on the sieve. She smooths down the mountain peak, her hands are as red as the paprika. And her shoes.

Pavel's tongue searches for the bits of nut stuck in his teeth, get in, says the man in the car, we're leaving.

The sun is resting on the mailboxes in the stairwell. The rambling roses cast shadows on the wall. Their flowers are small and grow in tight clumps.

The eye of the mailbox is not black and empty, it is white. A white mailbox eye is a letter from a soldier, a letter from Ilie. But Adina's name isn't on the envelope, just like it wasn't there the week before. Once again there is no stamp, no postmark, no sender. And once again inside the envelope is a torn piece of graph paper the size of a hand, with the same sentence in the same writing: I FUCK YOU IN THE MOUTH.

Adina crumples the envelope together with the note and feels dry paper sticking in her throat. The elevator is dark, no glowing green eye means no electricity. The stairwell smells of boiled cabbage. The nuts rattle as she walks. In the darkness Adina starts to count out loud, instead of the stairs she counts her left shoe and then her right. Each shoe raises and lowers itself, without her doing anything. Until every number is nothing more than her voice.

The bag with the nuts is on the kitchen table, the crumpled paper is on the nuts, next to the bag is an empty bowl. The drawer is half open, knife fork knife fork fork fork, together the tines make up a comb. Adina opens the drawer all the way, large knives and among them the hammer.

Her hand sets a nut on the table and the hammer hits it lightly. The nut has a crack, three firm blows and the shell breaks apart. And the brain inside the shell.

Cockroaches crawl over the stove. Seven reddish-brown large ones, four dark brown medium ones, nine small black ones the size of apple seeds. They don't crawl, they march. A soldier's summer for Ilie, no letter for Adina. On the other wall, inside her room, is a picture that is lit every morning by a band of light—Ilie in his uniform, hair like a hedgehog, grass straw in his mouth, shadow on his cheek, grass on his shoes. Every morning the whole day hangs suspended from this straw of grass.

Like Liviu, Ilie is in the flat land down south. The Danube is just as close and just as far from each, but they're in different places. In one place the Danube cuts off part of the country by flowing straight, in the other it cuts off part of the country by flowing crooked. In both places the shots being fired are the same, like a cracking branch, but different. Very different.

There are August days in this city when the sun is a peeled pumpkin that heats the asphalt from below and the concrete of the apartment blocks from above. Then it's so hot that heads pass through the day with the top of their skulls detached. At noon even the smallest thoughts crinkle up inside the heads and don't know where to go. Breath grows heavy in mouths. And all anyone is left with is a stray pair of hands used to press wet bedsheets against the windowpanes to cool things down. The sheets are already dry before the hands pull back from the glass.

It was on an August day like that when Ilie stood by the stove squashing cockroaches. But maybe it wasn't him at all, maybe it was the brutality of the heat inside his head. Death came with a crack for the large ones and silently for the small ones. Ilie counted only the large reddish-brown cockroaches that cracked.

When they're fully grown they turn red, said Ilie. Cockroaches will outlive everything, cities and villages and the endlessly plowed fields that have no lanes or trees. The miserable maize and the Carpathians and the wind on the stones, and sheep and dogs and humans. They will eat up all this socialism and lug it down to the Danube inside their fattened bellies. And the people on the other side will stand there horrified, blinking in the heat. And they'll shout across the water, that's the Romanians for you, they deserved it.

Then Ilie started sobbing and grabbed his face with hands that smelled of cockroach, and Adina dragged him out of the kitchen and gave him a glass of water. He held it in his hand but didn't drink. Disgusted and freezing despite the heat, he broke out in a cold sweat and pushed Adina away. He was so far removed from himself that he practically choked on his tongue when he said, the world is lucky to have the Danube.

Adina chews on a nut and looks out the window. The nut tastes bitter at first and then sweet. The sky is not looking down but is turned upward, its vast emptiness clinging to little spots of white, to letters that have all been read by the time it flees the city and escapes—a refugee above the city, bound for the Danube.

A child cries on the street below. Adina's tongue searches for the bits of nut stuck between her teeth. The shells lie scattered beneath the table.

A different silence

Where are the ball bearings, says the director. A brown moth the size of a fly flits out of his shirt collar and flutters past the geranium on the windowsill, looking for the factory yard below and behind the glass. Mara says, the ball bearings are on order. Outside the director's curtained window, on the other side of the geranium, shoes go clattering by. Heads of brown hair bob past. The potted geranium hovers first on one head then on the next. The geranium doesn't wave its red flowers, it just lets its leaves dangle motionless over the hair and point down into the sunken factory yard, into the rust, into the wire. The director doesn't see the heads of the people passing, only the tops of their hair. And he sees the moth at the windowpane. So, says the director, assuming the ball bearings are on order where are they. He steps so close to the glass that the open curtain brushes his forehead and the geranium grazes his chin. And the moth flips over and flutters past his shorn temples toward the meeting table. The ball bearings are on their way, Comrade Director, says Mara.

The director catches himself looking at the wire, out of

habit, but quickly pulls his face back away from the window. He isn't surprised by the moth. But he had not reckoned with a pair of tall shoes hitting the asphalt like a couple of broken bricks. Nor had he reckoned with short legs that don't bend as they walk. Or with a back so erect as if stiffened by wire.

These shoes, these legs, this back—all unsettle eyes that wish to remain blank. No matter how many years pass in the factory, no eye looks at the dwarf without seeing some reflection of itself. Without getting in its own way.

The director pulls back his head, his routine broken by the clatter walking with the dwarf.

A dwarf, and still he's made something of himself, says the director. Another person in his place would be begging on the street. He points at the small picture of the dictator in a frame on the table. A larger portrait hangs on the wall. Both show the black inside the eye. The two pictures look at each other, and their gazes meet between the wall and the table, right in front of the white curtain. Everyone who comes from HIS part of the country, says the director, has a strong will.

He means the south, the part of the country cut off by the Danube. The flat plain where the stony summers wither among the corn while it grows, and the stony winters freeze among the corn once it's forgotten. Where cushions of faded thistle fluff drift on the water. Where people count the floating cushions and know that for every person shot trying to escape, the Danube carries a cushion on its waves for three days, and for three nights shows a gleaming light under its waves, like a candle. The people in the south know the number of the dead, even if they don't know their names or faces.

Send a notice saying they're overdue, says the director. The ball bearings are on their way, says Mara. He rubs his neck against his shirt, his collar scratches. Every now and then, says the director, there's a knock at the door. Not very loud, I can barely hear it. And when I open the door I don't see anyone unless I look down right away. Then it turns out the foreman has sent the dwarf, and he doesn't say a word, just hands me a piece of paper. And then he leaves before I can say anything. I don't call after him because I can't ever remember his name. After all I can't call out, HEY DWARF. Mara smiles. You have nice legs, Mara, says the director. The geranium shakes. The director kneels on the carpet. Inside Mara's skirt his voice is deep. His hands are hard. Her thighs are hot. His teeth on her right thigh are distinct and wet and sharp. And from the portrait on the table, the black inside the eye watches. And blurs. Or is it the moth in the air, just a handbreadth away from Mara's eyes. Ouch, that hurts, Comrade Director, she says.

Every week the director comes to the gatehouse, the gatewoman told Clara. He doesn't come inside, doesn't cross the threshold. He just sticks his head in the door and pulls it right back out. He looks at the spools of wire and asks, what's the name of that dwarf. The gateman also looks at the wire because the director's eyes pull his own there, and because he believes that the director's head is completely entangled in the wire. Because whoever looks at the wire can't help getting fully entangled and is no longer able to listen. Everyone that is except for the gateman and myself, she told Clara, we look at the wire but don't see it anymore. So the gateman always gives the same answer: Comrade

Director, the dwarf's name is CONSTANTIN. He says it so loud I can hear him even if they're both off in the yard somewhere, said the gatewoman. And the director always says the same thing back, I try to memorize the name but I always forget it a second later, I can keep track of everything else but I never manage to hold on to the name of that dwarf. The gateman says, the dwarf belongs to the devil, otherwise he wouldn't be a dwarf. You know, the gatewoman told Clara, whenever the director's out in the yard a moth comes fluttering out of his shirt collar. As a young man he used to be the director of a hat factory, on the other side of the Carpathians. That's where the moths come from. After that he was director of a waterworks in the south and then a housing construction firm here in the city. But he's never managed to get rid of the moths from the hat factory. Anyway every time he asks about the dwarf's name he reaches into his bag and takes out a pen and a piece of paper and writes it down. He holds the paper and writes the name in big letters that fill the whole sheet, said the gatewoman. Then he puts pen and paper back in his bag and says, now I've got it. And the moth flies deep into the yard and gets lost in the wire. Then a week later the director once again sticks his head inside and says, what's the dwarf's name, I try to memorize the name but I always forget it a second later. And he takes out an identical piece of paper, and the same moth flies out of his shirt collar, and he writes down the same name all over again. And the moth flies deep into the yard, into the wire.

One time, the gatewoman told Clara, the director said that the same thing happens to the piece of paper as with the name of the dwarf—it disappears on its own.

Everybody in the factory knows the dwarf's name, said the gatewoman, because the name doesn't suit him at all. The director is the only one who can't remember that. He's always amazed that the dwarf's name is CONSTANTIN, and every time he says, that name doesn't suit the dwarf. It's because of the director I know the name CONSTANTIN doesn't suit him, she said. That never struck me before. But it strikes the director every time, she said. Which is why he ought to remember the name.

My son's also named Constantin, the gatewoman said to Clara, but I'd never connect his name with the dwarf because my child isn't a dwarf. And because the same name for a dwarf really isn't the same name at all. I've told my son he's not allowed to come looking for me in the factory, said the gatewoman. I'd never let him get caught up in all this wire. Because I know that if he ever started looking at the wire he'd never listen to me anymore. I'll never let my child become a worker here, not even for a single day.

The director kneels on the rug in front of Mara's knees that are no longer there. He sees the legs of the meeting table. He takes in more breath than his lungs can hold, he hyperventilates. His forehead feels salty and moist as though his face had two mouths, with the second feeling hot and in the wrong place, where his forehead reaches into his hair.

The striped cat sits under the meeting table and yawns. Her face is covered with fur. Sleep races through her dark stripes, her back, her stomach all the way into her paws. Her nose is black from the machine oil, blunt and old. But her teeth are sharp, white and young. Her face is furry, with thin stripes. Her eyes are alert, with the image of Mara's thigh fixed inside. And of a bite on the inner side, as large as a man's mouth.

The director stands up. The moth perches on the back of the chair. The director stands in front of the mirror. He doesn't know why, but he combs his hair.

In the workroom a worker is sprawled out on the oily floor. His eyes are half shut, his pupils have slid into his forehead. A puddle of blood has collected next to the press. The blood does not congeal, it is absorbed by the oil. The striped cat sniffs at the puddle. She twitches her whiskers and does not lick. Inside the worker's oily sleeve is a wrist without a hand. The hand is in the press. The foreman ties off the sleeve with a filthy rag.

The dwarf cradles the victim's head, warm and unconscious, in his hands. He keeps his hands still, because the hair on the man's head feels dead, and so does the skull under the hair and the brain under the skull. The upturned eyes peek out from under the lids, white like the rim of a cup. And under the eyes is a crease, which the dwarf stares at so long it seems to divide the unconscious face in two. And the cat's face, as well as his own face. Because when he keeps his hands so still, what feels dead creeps all the way up to his neck. The cat sniffs at the dwarf's hands and at his motionless chin. Her whiskers are tipped with red. But her eyes stay big and calm and do not squeeze out the image of Mara and the mouth-sized bite.

Someone calls out that the director is coming. Then Grigore and another man enter, a man no one knows. The man has clean hands and doesn't work at the factory. He asks for the name of the victim. The foreman says CRIZU.

The stranger kicks the cat out of the way and Grigore yells at the dwarf to get out of the way. The dwarf sticks his empty hands in his pockets and stands where the worker lay sprawled, out of the way for the others but not himself, and watches as Grigore and the stranger carry the unconscious man to the dressing room at the end of the floor. The body is heavy and soft. The smock hangs half open and billows out underneath.

Then the director comes through the open door and heads straight across the slippery floor to the dressing room. As he walks he shouts, don't just stand there, get back to work. A moth flies from his collar and gets lost by the windows where acacias hold back the light, because their trunks are already sprouting thin wooden shoots and random leaves. The director shuts the dressing room door behind him.

Then the stranger grasps the head of the worker while Grigore pries open his mouth and the director takes a hand flask out of his coat and pours brandy inside. After that the director washes his hands and turns the door handle and kicks open the dressing room door. The director and the stranger take the shortest slippery way out of the workroom into the yard, the spools of wire.

Grigore follows them out. And stops at the door and bumps against the dwarf. And shouts onto the shop floor, Crizu has been drunk since early this morning, Crizu was intoxicated at the workplace.

The dwarf leans out the workroom doorway and peers at the wire and eats a pear. His eyes are empty, his head is too big. Juice comes trickling out of his mouth as he utters the words, Crizu doesn't drink. Then the sun pulls a see-through cloud across its belly and the dwarf bites deep into the pear and chews. He chews the skin, the flesh, the core. His fingers are sticky, his shoes spattered. His hand is empty. But he doesn't swallow. His cheeks are full of chewed-up pear. Full up to the eyes.

Someone in the workroom says out loud, that doesn't matter, doesn't matter at all, then walks past the window and says, there's nothing anyone can do.

Disaster dangles from the mouth of whoever says those words like the leaves dangle from the tree outside the window. Whether summer green or autumn yellow, disaster is a branch in his face. The color is there, but not the leaves. Because disaster is always unadorned and as bare as winter wood. Whoever speaks like that has to avert his eyes from naked life. Has to close his mouth to naked speech before a thought forms in his head. Has to keep quiet and does not complain. And the dwarf has to eat and does not swallow. And Crizu has to swallow and does not drink.

But when the doctor comes and smells the brandy he says, it was Crizu's own fault that he fell down like that, drunk and unconscious.

A flock of sparrows shimmers through the yard. One bird separates and perches on a wire spool before settling on the ground. Then he hops until his wings have folded onto his back and his feathers are all smoothed out. After that the bird walks through the open door and heads straight across the slippery floor. The workers stand and watch. No one says a word.

Only the foreman stands at the press and bends over and

peers into a different silence, he is searching for the mangled hand.

While the dwarf stands in the yard on his tall half-brick shoes and chews his pear off into space.

Anca places all the pencils in the empty cola can. She wipes the dust off the empty beer can. And Mara stores all the pens in the empty beer can. And Eva waters the white-mottled vine and arranges its leaves below the picture on the wall. The picture shows blooming poppies. And David takes a pencil from the cola can. And Anca says the plant is called MOTHER-IN-LAW'S TONGUE. And David opens the notebook with the crossword puzzles. And Clara sets down the tiny brush and blows on her just-polished fingernails. And David says, the feeling after eating in four letters. And Anca calls out SICK. And Eva shouts DONE. And Mara shouts FULL.

Then the door opens, and Grigore comes into the office. And now for the third time that day Mara sets her foot on the chair and pulls up her skirt, to show Grigore her thigh. And Grigore holds her knee and looks at Mara's neck where a gold chain is dangling. What a crazy day, says Mara, the director bit me.

Eardrum infection

Face without face
Forehead of sand
Voice without voice
Nothing is left
Except for time

All Paul sees in the audience are eyes. The lights are out and all the eyes look alike, there are a hundred of them, and a few additional eyes belonging to the policemen.

Time without time
What can you change

The heads swaying to the beat of the song are different from the heads keeping watch. The crowd waves its hands, the hands hold flashlights pointed at the band, lighting up their faces. The singing turns to screaming. From the front row Anna can make out the little circles cast by the flashlights on the wall.

My only thought is this
What could I trade with you
One I call a brother
For a single cigarette

The side door is opened from the inside, a beam of light cuts into the auditorium. Dogs bark.

I've gone completely crazy
I went and fell in love
With someone who loves me
But my beloved's stupid
Since she does and since she doesn't
Really love me yet

And a man is dragged out through the beam of light, his back is arched as he is led away and the door is closed behind him.

My only thought is this
What could I sell to you
My coat is old and rumpled
With just one button left

The lead singer turns around and looks at Paul. Paul looks at Sorin, who taps Abi's arm with his drumstick.

Night comes and sews a sack
Sews a sack of darkness

The side door is opened from the outside, and heads wearing blue caps take their position in the beam of light. From where she sits in the middle of the auditorium Adina can see their bare ears sticking out from under their caps.

Stepmothergrass has bitter blades
The freight train whistles at the station

The bare ears listen to the sounds within, the dogs bark. Paul's mouth joins the chorus while his skull whirrs and his toes twitch. The flashlights glow. Then all the doors burst open, boots thunder inside. The stage goes dark and the auditorium goes bright. The screaming faces are suddenly naked in the glare. The policemen with their dogs and a man in a suit are standing in the auditorium. Paul plucks the strings of his guitar but there is no sound. Sorin's drumsticks too are mute. Because the man in the suit is standing on the stage right next to him shouting, the concert is over, calmly leave the hall.

Paul and Abi and Sorin join the lead singer but they no longer hear one another. Because the song has deflated with a gasp of fear. Fear as big as a mouth, as big as a pair of eyes. As big as the auditorium. And down in front of the stage, in the light, the policemen push, kick and club the singing crowd out through the open doors.

Little child where are your parents
Sitting on the asphalt is a barefoot shoe

The rubber truncheons seek out backs, heads, arms at random. Revolvers and machine pistols hang from leather straps. Adina leans against the wall. The rows of seats are empty. The policemen have had their fill of beating, the dogs their fill of barking. The only sound comes from the policemen's boots leaving the auditorium. Anna sits down between two empty seats in the front row. The dogs run after the boots.

The man in the suit stands onstage. Tomorrow, eight o'clock, Room Number 2, he says. Paul looks and says, understood. Abi asks why. Sorin coils a cable. Adina stands next to Sorin and watches the cable crawl up his arm. Anna sits on the edge of the stage, holding herself with both arms and staring out at the empty auditorium. And the man in the suit says, we're the ones who ask the questions. And Paul says, I'm on night duty. And the man in the suit jumps off the stage instead of using the steps and walks through the hall and shouts, then right after you get off work. He slams the door behind him. And Anna kisses Paul. And Paul says, go home, I'll go to your place tomorrow.

She presses her lips together. Stares at the ground and grinds her shoe against the floor. Paul says, I'll come after the interrogation, I'll be there for sure.

Anna walks past Adina, she has no eyes, just a narrow face. And cheeks warped with jealousy, from knowing that Adina lived with Paul for three years. She doesn't know what to do with her arms so she clasps her fingers together in order to keep going. Lifts each leg a little too high as she climbs down the stairs and into the auditorium. She walks past the empty seats. Slowly, so that her feet don't show how hard she's trying to save face by leaving before she gets edged out. Adina hears Anna's steps and watches Paul's eyes as they come back away from Anna's departure. Without turning around, Anna exits the auditorium through one of the side doors.

The bottle of brandy passes from one hand to the next. The voices jumble together. A beautiful evening. In a beautiful country. We can all hang ourselves. It's against the law to die together. Once we're dead we'll leave the hall calmly. I can write out our death certificates, says Paul. Sorin lifts the bottle to his lips and speaks into the bottle's neck, into the brandy sloshing against his teeth, please make sure mine lists my favorite cause of death: EARDRUM INFECTION.

Paul climbs down the stairs, Adina hops down next to them straight off the stage. Paul wanders between the empty chairs, taking the same path as Anna. Adina follows.

His jacket is so thin she can feel his ribs. The street is so dark that the sky itself is rustling, since the trees can't be seen. No cars, no people. The asphalt is cold and her soles are thin. Her throat is cold but the path is there, their shoes clatter. And the clattering creeps up to their cheeks. And just beyond Paul's cheek the stadium rises, quiet and tall, like a mountain. A mountain where the only ball in the air is the moon.

The hospital blocks the path with its black length and height. A few windows are lit, but only for themselves, they do not cast their glow into the night.

Take a look at all those windows, says Paul. Once I counted all one hundred and fifty-four of them. Last summer four people jumped. That doesn't matter, doesn't matter at all. If they don't jump out the windows they die in their beds. You'd think that would be more important than some song, too. For months we've been taking scraps from the stocking factory because we don't have any bandages or gauze.

Paul kisses Adina, clinging to her mouth. His hands are warm, she closes her eyes, feels his erection pressing against her. She pulls her lips away from his and rests her forehead against his neck. Stands there with her shoes between his, in the middle of the crossing, where the streets cut through each other during the day. His collar crinkles in her ear. But her ears are not with her head, they're back with the barking dogs. And her eyes are up there with the running moon, searching for holes in the clouds.

You better go now, says Adina.

Then she walks across the asphalt, taking small steps, but there's nothing there. Just the clatter of her shoes and the heat in her forehead to guide her way. When she reaches the curb she turns around. Paul hasn't moved, he lingers in the crossing like a shadow, his face a little lighter than the rest of him. He follows her with his eyes.

Then he makes his way toward the lit windows. The wind lifts his hair, the air smells like wet earth and freshly mown grass.

Behind the hospital is a forest. Except it isn't. It's a tree nursery that's been allowed to go wild. The trees are older than the housing blocks that huddle together on the outskirts of town, older than the hospital. It's still possible to make out the original rows by looking at the bases of the trees and focusing on the few straight trunks that remain. But at treetop level the needles and leaves are all stitched together, and the mix changes daily. What hasn't changed in years is the thicket behind the hospital where no one tree matches another. And that the patients from the upper floors can see this better than anyone else and that they are disturbed. Paul knows they spend hours staring at the thicket through a pair of binoculars. And that as they do they become monosyllabic, like forest rangers.

It started with a sick forest ranger from the West Carpathians and it never stopped. He was up on the tenth floor. Another ranger from the same forest came to visit and brought him a pair of binoculars. To pass the time, he said. So the sick ranger and the men on the tenth floor started spending their days watching the forest. Until the sick ranger died. When the ranger who had brought the binoculars came with the widow and a coffin, he took the man's dentures, glasses, nail clipper and hat. But he left the binoculars for the others. And little by little, because they were so attached to the binoculars, they started turning into sick rangers, every one of them, all the way down to the third floor. Now each floor has a timetable that lists when and for how long a given patient may watch the forest.

Once Paul looked at the thicket through the binoculars. He wanted to know what the sick rangers saw. Paul knows the forest because he often walks there after work. Nevertheless he was startled by the giant ball of needles and leaves. And by the helter-skelter undergrowth. And by how the trunks and branches had adapted, as the wild growth chased away whatever was restrained by cultivation, cutting off the light from above and claiming the ground below. The grass, too, was closer in binoculars than it ever is under a pair of shoes.

The sick rangers also said they saw dogs and cats. And men and women coupling in the darker places or in the clearings in the fading twilight. And children stuffing grass in each other's mouths in the mornings and playing hide-and-seek and forgetting all about the game when they realize no one is looking for them.

Paul hears these children now and then because they climb over three rows of barbed wire into the hospital yard to get to the rusty windowless ambulance cars, and what they're looking for is pain.

The smallest man carries the biggest cane

The windshield is covered with thick dust.

Her hair is caught under his elbow. His mouth pants as his belly thrusts. She presses her face against the back of the seat. She can hear his watch ticking. The ticking smells of hurried roads, lunch breaks, gasoline. His underwear is on the floor, his pants are draped over the steering wheel. The cornstalks outside are leaning into the window, peering at her face. Her panties are under his shoe.

The silk on the ears is torn and brittle. The leaves give off a dry rattle, the stalks are twiggy and lean and knock against one another. Between the tassels grows colorless sky.

She closes her eyes. The colorless sky above the cornfield breaks into her forehead.

Something clatters outside the car.

She opens her eyes at once and sees a bicycle propped against a cornstalk. A man in the field shoulders a sack and carries it to the bicycle. Someone's coming, she says.

The cornstalks knock against the man's head.

Clara's panties have a tread mark left by the shoe. She puts them on. He won't bother us, says Pavel, he's stealing corn. Clara looks at his watch. The man wheels his bicycle through the dry cornstalks.

I have to get back to the factory, says Clara. Pavel tugs his pants off the steering wheel, sunflower seeds drop from his pocket onto his bare knee, how long can you be gone from the courthouse, asks Clara.

The car hums, gray from all the dust. I don't work at the courthouse, says Pavel. Clara's dress is crumpled, her back wet with sweat. Aren't you a lawyer, asks Clara. Yes, he says, but not at the courthouse. The sky broadens because the corn is now running in the opposite direction, what's left is a low, rattling field that stretches to the horizon. I saw you in a different car, says Clara. He looks out the window and asks, where. By the cathedral, on the street next to the park, the car was black. She sees the sunflower seeds scattered between his shoes. Pavel turns the wheel so lightly his hands don't seem to do a thing. There are black cars in every factory, he says. She sees the seconds ticking on his watch, but you don't work in a factory.

He says nothing and shrugs his shoulders. And Clara says nothing and looks out the window.

In Clara's factory there is a corner where the sky closes all vision, where a bright weariness lurks day after day, waiting to climb into the city. Into the lunch breaks and the empty afternoon days. A weariness that closes the eyes somewhere between the wire and the rust. That throbs in the head when the gateman's hand is rummaging through a bag. A weariness that places the same aged faces opposite each other in the streetcar between the stops. A weariness that enters an apartment before the person returning home, the way eyes can enter before the head. And that stays in the apartment until the day comes to an end, somewhere between the door to the apartment and the window that looks outside.

Clara looks at Pavel's temples. And what if I think the worst, she says.

Caught in the glass, Pavel's birthmark is black like the fresh molehills in the grass outside the windshield.

The car searches out the potholes in the road. Pavel tugs on his reddish-blue flecked tie. One of Clara's hairs is caught on his collar. She picks it off with her fingertips. Pavel presses his neck against her hand and asks, what is it. She says, nothing, a hair. What will you tell your wife. The lane of poplars flies up along the roadside. He says, nothing. How old is your daughter. He says, eight. The poplars drop yellow leaves on both sides of the road. Clara's fingers become uncertain and drop the hair.

I know what I know, says Pavel.

A crow sits in the wheatgrass, glossy, gleaming.

Next to the room with the loudspeaker is a little escape ladder leading up to the attic. The ladder has thin iron rungs. Clara follows Eva's heels as they climb. Mara, Anca and Maria are already there. The undersized attic window isn't fully closed, just ajar. Eva pushes it all the way open. Down below, on the other side of the yard, are three stairs and an open door. Behind the door is a corridor that connects the men's changing room on the left with their showers on the right.

Mara's hair is right in Eva's face. Anca's shoulder is digging into Maria's back, Maria's barrette is scratching Clara's ear.

The men climb up the stairs in their work smocks like they do every day, then they walk down the corridor and go into the door on the left. A while later they reemerge naked and walk across the corridor to the door on the right that leads to the showers. The steam from the hot water clouds the corridor. But from May through September the late afternoon sun falls across the factory yard at just the right angle to hit both the stairs and the corridor. Then the light pierces the steam and the naked men are fully visible as they pass from one door to the other.

The naked men scrunch their feet as they walk, stepping gingerly with knotty toes, because the concrete floor is always wet and cold and slippery. They have fat stomachs and withered backs and hunch their shoulders. Their bellies are covered with hair, their thighs thin. Their pubic hair forms thick knots. Their testicles cannot be seen from the attic window. Only their dangling penises.

Blond men have such white cocks, says Mara. Eva leans on Mara's back and says, all Moldavians have white cocks. Not old George, says Maria. I haven't seen his yet, says Clara. Her bangs get in her eye, she brushes them back and discovers a thread of corn silk. Eva says, George just went up the stairs, he'll come out soon. Mara raises her face above Eva's. Her eyes are big. Clara lets the corn silk fall to the floor.

The dwarf, says Maria, my God, the dwarf has the biggest of all. The shortest man carries the biggest cane.

Clara stands on her tiptoes.

The grass straw in the mouth

A woman stands in the window in the apartment opposite Adina's, watering her petunias. She's no longer young but not yet old, Paul said about her years ago, when he still lived with Adina. Even then the woman had chestnut-red hair done up in big waves. And the windowpane already had a slanted crack. Five years have passed without leaving any mark on the woman's face. Her hair hasn't stiffened or grown paler. And every year the white petunias are different and yet the same.

Back then the white petunias were already drooping, all the woman could see when she watered were their bent stems. She couldn't see their white funnels.

People who looked up from the street and saw little spots of white high among the windows and didn't know they were petunias thought they were seeing children's socks or handkerchiefs, fluttering in the summer breeze all the way into the fall.

Adina stands on the fox pelt in front of her half-opened wardrobe. She's looking for her gray wool skirt. Her skirts are all on hangers, the thin summer ones in front of the winter skirts. When the seasons change, the clothes switch places in the wardrobe, and Adina can see how long Ilie's been away. His clothes don't change hangers or drawers or shelves. They just lie there as though he were no longer alive. A picture on the wall shows him standing with his shoes in the grass. But the grass doesn't belong to him and the shoes don't belong to him. Nor do his pants, jacket or cap.

One day two summers ago a loud voice called up to Adina from down below. Adina went to the window. Ilie was standing on the other side of the housing settlement, below the apartment with the petunias. He lifted his head and shouted: who are they blooming for. And Adina shouted back: for themselves.

Adina steps into her gray skirt. Her foot slips on the fox's tail, which slides away from the rest of the fur. The tail has come off where the stripe running down the back is the lightest, right where it tapers into a narrow point. Adina turns the fur over and examines the underside, the skin is as white and wrinkled as old dough. The fur on top and the skin below are warmer than the floor, and warmer than her hands.

It's rotted off, decayed, thinks Adina. She shoves the tail against the fur so it looks like the tail has grown back. From the picture frame, in the clothes that don't belong to him, with eyes that aren't his own, Ilie watches her hands. In his mouth he has a grass straw.

Rot and decay are wet, thinks Adina. But a fur dries out, just like a grass straw. In the picture the grass straw is the only thing that belongs to Ilie. The grass straw makes his face look old.

Adina goes into the kitchen. From that window too she sees the woman watering her white petunias.

The petunias open in the morning when the light comes and close in the evening when the sky turns gray. They have a clock inside that measures dark and light. Every day they wind their funnels open and shut, until finally they overwind them right into October.

A knife is lying on the kitchen table, next to some quince peels and half a quince. The side that's cut open has dried in the air just like the underside of fox fur, and the flesh is as brown as the hairs from the fox. A cockroach is nibbling at the snake made of quince peels.

To peel a quince like that you would have to hold the quince in one hand and a knife in the other, Adina thinks. You'd have to peel a quince and then you would have to eat some of the peeled quince, which would pucker your gums. You would have to bite, chew, swallow and close your eyes until the quince traveled all the way from your hand into your stomach.

Adina lays her hands on the kitchen table and lays her face on top of them. She holds her breath.

You'd have to remember that no one would ever leave half a quince just lying there, otherwise it would dry out like a fur, or like a grass straw. And if you ate a whole quince, if an entire quince had traveled from hand to stomach, Adina says to her hands on the table, then you would open your eyes and be a different person.

A woman who never eats quince like that.

Face without face

The tape plays in one room what is being recorded in another. A deep voice comes through the speaker on the desk. The deep voice says, so, KACHONI, how do you pronounce that. KARÁCSONYI, says a quiet voice. So it's Hungarian, says the deep voice, does it mean something in Hungarian. Christmas, says the quiet voice. The deep voice laughs.

Pavel leafs through a file, tilts a photograph into the light, and laughs. He laughs longer and louder than the deep voice.

First name, says the deep voice. ALBERT, says the quiet voice. What about ABI, asks the deep voice. That's what my friends call me, says the quiet voice. And your father, says the deep voice. He called me ABI too, he's no longer alive, says the quiet voice. And the deep voice becomes like the quiet one and says, I see. When did he die. And the quiet voice becomes like the deep voice and says, you already know when. The deep voice asks, what makes you think that. And the quiet voice says, because you are asking. It's the other way around, says the deep voice, if we already know something then we don't ask. A lighter clicks in the speaker. Back then I was in kindergarten, says the deep voice, just like you. Your father was also named ALBERT, just like you. Do you remember him. No, says the quiet voice. First you said your father called you ABI, says the deep voice, and now you say you don't remember him. That's a contradiction. That's not a contradiction, says the quiet voice, my mother also calls me ABI. What do you want from me.

But right at the beginning you said that only your friends call you ABI, says the deep voice. That's also a contradiction. You see, KACHONI, I can't pronounce your last name. You see, ALBERT, all these contradictions are connected. The deep voice becomes like the quiet one. Or can I call you ABI like your friends, says the deep voice. No, says the quiet voice. Well there was nothing uncertain about that, says the deep voice. What do you want from me, asks the quiet voice.

Pavel holds a photo under the lamp. It's old, not shiny, with just a few stripes of light that fade off into a sky where everything is empty. Because where the sky stops is a wall, and leaning against the wall is a man with sunken cheeks and large ears. Pavel writes a date on the back of the photo.

The deep voice coughs. Paper crinkles in the speaker. For instance here, says the deep voice, which now becomes like the quiet voice: I've gone completely crazy, I went and fell in love, with someone who loves me, but my beloved's stupid, since she does and since she doesn't, really love me yet. That's also a contradiction, all these contradictions are connected. That's just a song, the quiet voice says, now a little louder.

Pavel glances at his watch and puts the photo back in the file. He turns the speaker off and shoves the drawer shut. He picks up the phone, just beyond the window is a poplar. He looks outside, his eyes are small, his gaze as wet as the poplar. His eyes pierce through the poplar branches but don't see them. He turns the dial twice and says, we're not getting anywhere, it's almost four o'clock.

Pavel remains silent for a moment, he looks through the poplar, the wind blows, the leaves are wet, his lighter clicks. The cigarette glows. He blows smoke in front of him and shuts the door.

Write, says the voice. The eyes in the forehead are light brown. They shift back and forth and go dark. The eyes are reading from a sheet of paper on top of a finger-thick folder. The poplar tree is swaying outside. The mouth between the telephone and the desk lamp is moving. Abi's gaze latches on to the windowpane. Rain is falling outside the window, but Abi can't see the raindrops hitting the poplar, as though the poplar wasn't there. All he can see are the little balls of water dripping off the leaves and dropping to the ground. Abi squeezes the pen with his fingers. The bulb hanging from the ceiling is so bright it sends threads of light thrashing this way and that. Abi stares at the bare tabletop. The pen doesn't belong to him nor does the blank sheet of paper. The voice screams and thrashes just like the light threads. Below the voice, in the fold of the chin, is a small razor cut. The cut is a few days old.

The door opens slowly. The eyes between the telephone and the desk lamp are half-closed. They don't look up because they know who's entering.

From the edge of the desk Abi does look up from the blank paper without letting go of the pen. The man with the reddish-blue flecked tie walks to the desk, looks at the blank paper and holds out his hand. As Abi extends his own hand, still wrapped around the pen, he sees a birthmark between the man's shirt collar and his ear. The man says, PAVEL MURGU and shakes Abi's hand together with the pen.

Face without face, in other words he lost his face, says the razor cut, raising his hand to his forehead. Forehead of sand, in other words a head with no brains. Voice without voice, so no one is listening, says the razor cut. The birthmark takes a seat next to the razor cut and gazes out through the windowpane.

Maybe the man with the birthmark is looking at the poplar, after all he can afford to do that, his mind is free to leave here and go somewhere else, thinks Abi. Because the man's light brown eyes are wide open and hard and they shine as they look at Abi, taking in the face that belongs to Abi and not them, Abi's cheeks, Abi's fingertips, the little breaths that Abi's mouth snatches from the glaring light.

It's a contradiction, Abi thinks, that someone dies but doesn't have a grave. And it's also a contradiction that he would be the one to have to say that. And that his throat is pounding but his mouth doesn't move. And it's a contradiction when you're the son of a dead man and you arrive in a city that really is a prison and when you look for something callused or something broken in everyone who lives there—but find nothing but the ordinary. Ordinary eyes, ordinary steps, ordinary hands, ordinary bags. In the display windows the ordinary wedding photos, the bridal veil cascading over the grass in the park like foam from a waterfall. And next to it the white shirt in the black suit like snow on slate. And it's a contradiction when the son of a dead man gets frightened because these ordinary men and women meet each other on the streets of this city and instead of asking HOW ARE YOU they ask HOW ARE YOU GETTING ALONG WITH LIFE.

Face without face, who does that refer to, asks the man with the birthmark.

And it's a contradiction, Abi thinks, that between being starved and being beaten the prisoners were forced to fashion their guilty verdict into cabinets and chairs for a furniture factory when they had no beds themselves, only knotty wood and knotty fingers. And that newlyweds bought cabinets and chairs that had been glazed and upholstered by those hands, whether they knew it or not. The dizzying height of the sky above the prison is a contradiction as well. And the fact that it was there back then, looking straight down on the city in a cold swath of sunlight, where crows dive quietly and slowly into the roofs.

It doesn't refer to anybody, says Abi, it's just a song. And the razor cut says, then why do you sing it if it doesn't refer to anybody. Because it's a song, says Abi.

It refers to our country's president, says the birthmark. No, says Abi.

The walls are full of outlets. The outlets have mouths. The base of the lamp has yellow numerals, inventory numbers.

I see you aren't informed, says the birthmark. You see, your friend Paul has confessed, and he should know. After all he's the one who wrote the song, says the chin cut.

There are yellow inventory numbers marking the side of the desk and the door to the cabinet. Paul can't have confessed, says

Abi, because it isn't true. The birthmark laughs and the telephone rings. The razor cut holds the receiver to his cheek and says: no, yes, what, how's that. Fine. The mouth whispers something to the birthmark, whose face is bright in the light but shows no emotion.

The razor cut says, as you see, your friend Paul doesn't tell you everything.

It's now dark outside, the poplar is gone. The lightbulb, the ceiling, the cabinet and the wall, the outlets and the door are reflected in the glass. A room shrunk into half a window, with no one inside.

So write down who it does refer to, says the birthmark. And the razor cut says, if we're satisfied you can go. And if we're not you'll stay and think, says the birthmark. The razor cut clutches the file under his arm. The birthmark stands at the door and blows smoke out of his nose. You'll think better on your own, says the razor cut. He spits on his fingertips and counts out five white pages. His light brown eyes are round and happy. There's more than enough paper, he says.

By the way in that song of yours that doesn't refer to anybody there's a line I like very much, about night sewing a sack of darkness, says the birthmark.

The door closes from outside. The keys rattle in the door. The floor stretches out in the light. The cigarette smoke drifts to the dark window. Otherwise nothing moves: not the empty desk or the chair or the cabinet or the sheets of paper. Or the window.

It's a contradiction, thinks Abi, that outside on the wet street, this window is nothing but a window. That every day and every night the world is divided into those who interrogate and torture and those who keep silent. And it's a contradiction that one summer day, in a farmyard in front of a rusted bathtub planted with geraniums, right next to the beehive, a child asks his mother where his father is. And that the mother raises the child's arm and takes his hand in hers and bends his little fingers and points one at the sky and says: up there, do you see. And that the child looks up for just a moment and sees nothing but sky while his mother stares at the geraniums in the bathtub. That the child sticks his outstretched finger into the narrow slit of the beehive until his mother says, don't do that, you'll wake the queen. That the child asks, why is the queen asleep, and his mother says because she's so tired. It's a contradiction that the child removes his finger because he doesn't want to wake the tired queen and then he asks what his father's name is. And that the mother says: his name was ALBERT.

Abi writes on the empty sheet:

KARÁCSONYI ALBERT
Mother MAGDA née FURÁK
Father KARÁCSONYI ALBERT

His hand doesn't feel itself. Inside a dark half-window is Room Number 2. The lightbulb burns. No one is there. Only three names on a sheet of paper.

Pavel opens the door to a different room. A woman's eyes watch from behind the desk. The woman is holding a pen. A sheet of paper is lying on the desk, blank except for three short names in crooked writing. Let's see, says Pavel. He picks up the paper and reads.

His hands fly, the chair stumbles. The woman's head bangs against the wardrobe. Her eyes stay big and rigid. The lower lashes are thin and wet. The upper ones thick and dry and bent upward like grass. The door shuts from the outside.

Inside the woman's eyes the wardrobe is curved. The room is so still that the objects lie down in the light. The woman is lying on the floor in front of the wardrobe. Her shoe is lying under the chair.

Shrunk into a dark half-window, Room Number 9 is all lit up. And no one is there.

Pavel opens the garden gate. The birch trunks gleam against the black grass. His keys rattle in front of the house. Before Pavel can unlock the door his wife opens it from inside.

She smells of kitchen vapors, he kisses her cheek. She carries his briefcase into the kitchen. His daughter's forehead comes up to his belt, the tip of his tie. Pavel lifts her up, Father your hair is wet, she says, and slides down his front.

Pavel opens his briefcase, the buckles are cold with condensation. He takes out a package of Jacobs coffee, a tub of breakfast margarine and a jar of Nutella and places them on the kitchen counter next to the television. A worker's chorus is singing, he turns down the volume. He counts out twelve packs of cigarettes and sets them on the refrigerator next to the white porcelain dog. The head of the warehouse is out of town on business, he says, he'll be back tomorrow, I'll send someone to fetch the veal. He lays the Alpenmilch chocolate on top of the apples in the fruit bowl. One of the apples rolls off, Pavel catches it. His daughter holds her hand out for the chocolate. Her father asks, how was school. Her mother stirs the pot and says, no chocolate, we're about to eat. And she looks at Pavel as she raises the spoon to her mouth and says to the quivering blob of fat, her grades aren't going to get any better because of chocolate.

Pavel looks at the television screen. A woman and a man are standing in front of the workers' chorus. They tilt their heads forward and scamper around with their feet, then tilt their heads back and scamper around with their feet.

I've been telling you for a month, says the mother, you have to go to the school and talk with the teacher. Everyone takes her coffee, says the daughter, except for us. And you can see that in her grades, says the mother.

She slurps the blob of fat off the spoon. On the television screen the man trips offstage to the left and the woman trips off to the right. Pavel drapes his jacket over the back of the chair.

The teacher's not getting any coffee. At most a black eye. After I'm done talking with her she'll be bringing coffee to us.

A drop of soup splashes onto the table. Veal my foot, says the mother. Maybe seven years ago it would have counted as a calf, but that meat's been cooking for hours and still isn't soft. That was an old cow. The daughter laughs and taps her spoon against the soup bowl. A parsley leaf sticks to her chin. The mother picks a bay leaf out of the soup and places it on the edge of the bowl. And my shoes won't be ready before Christmas, she says. Actually my shoes are ready, just not for me. Today the school inspector came by the factory with his wife. She took two pairs. First she wanted brown, but changed her mind and wanted gray.

Then she didn't like the black ones and wanted white with buckles. The black ones were supposed to be mine, made of patent leather. But in the end those were the ones that fit. So now they're hers.

The daughter has made herself a mustache from a piece of meat. Pavel licks a parsley leaf off his fingertip. And the inspector, he asks the mother. She looks at the daughter's mustache and says, he told everyone that he has two corns, one on his middle toe and one on his little toe.

On the television screen the president of the country strolls through a factory hall. Two female workers present him with bouquets of carnations. The workers applaud, their lips open and close in time to their clapping. Pavel hears himself saying, there are black cars in every factory. And he hears Clara saying, but you don't work in a factory. He reaches around and switches off the television.

The mother says, for three hours our director was kneeling next to the chair where the inspector's wife was sitting. His eyes were watery and his mouth twisted and soft. His hands were two shoehorns, all they did for three whole hours was shovel her heels into different shoes. He could no longer straighten his fingers. And in between fittings he was kissing her hand. You should see her calves. Pavel pulls a fiber of meat from between his teeth. The daughter rummages through her father's briefcase. She shakes three thick drops out of a perfume bottle onto her hand. Her calves are like a fattened pig's, says the mother, no patent leather shoes are going to help that. She ought to wear rubber boots. The mother sniffs the daughter's hand, Chanel, she says, then picks up the porcelain dog from the refrigerator. After that the workers acted out Director and Madame, says the mother, rolling their pants up to their knees and walking back and forth in high heels to show how Madame tried on shoes.

Pavel's eyes are tired, the meat sticks to his fork. The daughter's face is smeared with chocolate, which rings her mouth like dirt. She cries. Her father props his head in his hands, his forehead feels heavy. Stuffed handkerchiefs in their pant legs to show her calves, then climbed up on the table and draped curtains over their hair, he hears his wife saying. And at the same time he doesn't hear her because he's hearing the cornfield rattling in the middle of his forehead. And Clara's voice saying, And what if I think the worst.

So then the director came bursting through the door, says the mother, and told them they could all expect disciplinary action. Including the women who were watching and laughing. Including me. Pavel hears Clara's laughter in the middle of his forehead. He takes his wife's hand in his own. She presses her mouth against his ear. The kiss floods his neck, his cheeks, his forehead. He hears his voice telling Clara, I don't work at the courthouse.

His wife's ear is next to his mouth like a young rolled-up leaf. I was planning on giving you the perfume this evening, Pavel says into the ear. And he doesn't hear himself.

He hears himself telling Clara, I know what I know.

The razor blade

The stadium is enclosed by an earthen wall. The grass has been so eroded by the autumn that soil shows between the blades. Also rocks. The apartment blocks in the housing settlement beyond the stadium are squeezed together, from across the empty parking lot they seem no higher than the shrubs that reach up along the earthen wall—lilacs, mock orange and rose of Sharon that are never pruned because they don't venture over the wall itself. The plants sneak into bloom early, and by spring the flowers have faded and summer growth is already well under way. But now they stand naked on the earthen wall, shaking their twigs and branches, unable to shelter anything from the gusting wind.

The long-distance runner over the entrance to the stadium is nothing but a picture painted on stone. But during the bare season there are no hurdles to slow him down. When the branches have no leaves, the long-distance runner is a winner. He looks down at the bread line in front of the store, at the screaming faces and the thick padded clothes, but he doesn't feel hungry. Over the stadium the sun has turned away, a ring of milky white that gives no warmth. But the long-distance runner doesn't feel the cold. With naked calves he runs overhead, past the little people and into the city.

A car pulls up to the parking lot. Two men wearing windbreakers climb out. One is young, the other older. They glance briefly at the blind sun. Their pant legs flutter as they hurry across the lot, their shoes shine. They're eating sunflower seeds and spitting the black shells onto the well-worn path that leads them, the older man followed by the younger, between the garbage bins and mountains of empty boxes, toward the apartment blocks of the housing settlement.

The older man takes a seat on a bench, looks up at the windows and munches his sunflower seeds. Behind him, high up, is the window with the petunias. The younger man points out a window in a building on the other side of the settlement the same height as the petunias and says, that's her apartment. One room and a kitchen. The room is in front, that's where the fox fur is, the young man says, the kitchen is off to the side.

The wind sweeps over the bench. The older man rubs his legs and turns up his collar.

The younger man unlocks the door. His key does not rattle. He bolts the door from inside. He doesn't trip over the shoes in the entrance hall, he knows exactly where they are, the sandals with the black traces of her toes. The bed is unmade, the nightgown folded on the pillow.

He goes to the window. The woman with the chestnut-red hair done up in big waves is standing behind her petunias. He signals to her with his hand. He crosses to the wardrobe, kneels on the floor. He takes a razor blade out of his jacket's inner pocket. He unpacks the razor blade and places the paper wrapper next to his knee. He slices the right hind leg off the fox. Then he licks his fingertip and wipes the cut hair from the floor. He rubs the hair between his thumb and forefinger into a firm ball and drops it into his jacket pocket. He wraps the razor blade in the paper and sticks it in his inner pocket. He slides the cut-off leg back against the belly of the fox.

He stands up and checks to see if the cut is visible. He goes to the bathroom. He lifts the toilet cover. He spits into the toilet. He pisses and closes the cover without flushing. He goes to the door of the apartment and unlocks it. He quickly sticks his head into the hall and steps out. He locks the apartment door.

The petunias are whiter than the sun's milky ring. They will soon freeze. The bench down below is vacant. The ground in front of the bench is strewn with sunflower seeds.

Two men walk along the well-worn path that leads them, the younger man followed by the older, between the garbage bins and mountains of empty boxes. They cross the parking lot. The shrubbery climbs the earthen wall, higher and higher, into the bare season.

A fox will step into a trap

The gateman paces up and down at the entrance to the factory, his coat draped over his shoulders. The sun casts a cold light on his face. As he waits to inspect the bags he eats sunflower seeds. His coat drags on the ground.

Mara comes out of the main shop floor, having brought three knives for David. The blades are freshly sharpened. David uses one to cut through a bacon rind and doesn't wipe it off. So the gateman won't see it was just sharpened, he says, placing it in his bag. He puts the other two knives in the drawer, I'll take one tomorrow and the other the day after, he says.

Eva rinses out the water glasses, her fingers squeak on the wet surface. The dwarf doesn't have to sweep the hall today, says Mara, so he'll be one of the first to get to the showers, we better hurry. Anca grabs her purse without buttoning her coat.

David buttons his coat and takes his bag.

David walks to the gate carrying the greasy knife in his bag. Mara, Eva and Clara walk past the giant spools into the rear yard, a flock of sparrows comes fluttering out of the wire. The attic window below the edge of the roof is ajar.

Clara feels a knot in her throat, her tongue rises to her eyes. She gags, her eyes lose focus. When she looks up, the attic window is a string of windows suspended in the air. Mara and Eva are far ahead, past the spools, perhaps already on the rungs of the iron ladder.

At least for a few more days, as long as the sun casts its cold light on these stairs even just for a moment, the eyes of the three women gather in the attic window every afternoon at four o'clock. Soon the sun will no longer touch the staircase at all. It will move across the wall, dull and pale, in far too narrow an arc. And then for months the steam in the little hallway outside the shower will be so blindingly thick no eye can see through it. The women's curiosity does not subside right away, for another few days it climbs into the women's heads and the women keep climbing the iron rungs. They crowd around the window, waiting in vain for the light that no longer comes. By the time the first men enter the shower the sun has already stolen past the wall. The women look at one another. They turn around, jammed so close together they seem to have no arms. Then they give up. Mara quietly closes the attic window and slides the little rusty latch. For several months the window will stay locked.

Down in the yard Clara bends over, props her head against a wire spool and straddles the rusty path. She vomits bread and bacon. Her hands are cold, she wipes her mouth with her handkerchief. She glances up at the attic window, Eva's and Mara's heads are a blur, Clara can't make out their faces. The striped cat sits down twice between Clara's shoes, eating what she threw up, even licking the wire. Her stripes come floating out of her fur.

Adina leans against the bare acacia by the factory entrance, the wire spools are stacked higher than the fence, smoke rises from the gatehouse chimney but does not fray above the crooked street, the gray wool rises and then falls back on the roof. The wind carries steam from the brewery, the air smells like cold sweat, the cooling tower is cut off by the clouds.

Two weeks ago the officer's wife gave the servant's daughter a coat with a fox fur collar, with two legs for tying under the chin. The legs have little paws and brown, shiny claws. The steam from the brewery smells like the fox collar, which had made Adina sneeze. The servant's daughter said it was naphthalene. If a fur doesn't smell like naphthalene, she said, come summer the fox rot will eat right through the pelt. And then the hair doesn't just fall off one strand at a time, it stays on the hide as though it were still growing and waits. Then just when you go to pick up the fur it comes off in big clumps like sudden hair loss. And you're left holding a bare hide, like skin on bones, all covered with tiny sandy grains, with grit. The servant's daughter smiled and fingered the paws of her fox collar.

Clara approaches the gate. The gatewoman is holding the cat on her lap, stroking its striped fur. David's knife is on the table, the gateman saw that it had been freshly sharpened in the factory. The gateman's coat slips off his shoulder, his hand sticks Clara's gummed-up handkerchief quickly back into her purse. A truck rattles through the gate, the wheels rattle as it moves onto the street, and the stacked wire spools rattle above and below as well. The driver's face jiggles in the rearview mirror. Farther away is the white curtain of haze from the brewery. Through the rattling Clara hears someone calling her name.

Adina walks through a cloud of dust. Her kiss lands just under Clara's eye, her hands are blue from the cold wind, her nose is damp. Let's go to my place right away, she says, I have to show you something.

Clara bends over and picks up all the pieces of the fox fur, gray light falls through the window. The empty table is dark and shiny. Everything I need to eat is in the kitchen, Adina says, bread, sugar, flour. Clara runs her fingertips over the fox's tail, then over the cut on the leg. They can poison me whenever they want, says Adina. Clara sets the fur back on the floor. Without taking off her coat she sits on the unmade bed and stares at the gap between the fox's belly and its right hind leg, at the empty band of floor the width of her hand. She shoves the tail against the rest of the fur, it looks as if it were growing there, the cut is completely invisible.

Clara's thin, pointy fingers peek out of her coat sleeves, the red dabs of nail polish shine. Adina rests her hands on the table and kicks off her shoes. When Clara moves her hands it's easy to see the rust stains on the inside of her fingers.

I was just about ten years old, Adina tells Clara, when my mother took me to a nearby village to buy that fur. We crossed the bridge without water, the one the slaughterhouse workers use every morning. But on that morning the sky wasn't red, it was heavy and all torn up. The men on the bridge didn't have red cockscombs. It was a few days before Christmas, there was frost everywhere but no snow. Only a little dusting here and there, flakes whirling in the wind, in the furrows on the field. I was so anxious and excited I hadn't slept the whole night. I'd wanted a fox for so long that the joy of getting it the next day was half turned to fear. The morning was icy cold and there wasn't a single sheep out. And I thought as we were walking that where there aren't any sheep out there can't be any village. The field was flat, with just a few low bushes, so the sky seemed to come at us from all directions. It came all the way down to my mother's headscarf and I was afraid we'd lost our way. I walked and walked but didn't get tired. Maybe sleepy, because I felt a tired tickling in my forehead, but that tiredness kept me going. When we reached the village there wasn't anyone on the street. All the windows had Christmas trees. Their branches were so close to the windowpanes that you could make out the individual needles, as if they'd been set up for the people passing by outside and not the people in the house. And since no one else was passing by, they were there just for my mother and me. My mother didn't realize it, though. But I carried those trees with me, from one window to the next, all by myself.

Then we stopped. My mother knocked on a window. I still remember that it didn't have any Christmas tree. We went into the yard. And then down a long open walkway where you couldn't see the walls on account of all the fox furs.

After that we went in the main room, which had a cast-iron stove and a bed, no chair. The hunter came inside carrying one of the pelts. He said, this is the biggest one. He slid his hands under the fox so that the legs hung down while he moved the arms. The legs shook like they were running. And behind the legs the tail wiggled as if it belonged to a different, smaller animal. I asked if I could see his rifle. The hunter laid the fox on the table and smoothed out its fur. He said, you don't shoot a fox. A fox will step into a trap. The man's hair and beard and the hairs on his hands were as red as the fox. His cheeks too. Even back then, fox and hunter were one and the same.

Clara takes off her coat and steps out of the room. In the bathroom she gags and throws up. Adina looks at the coat lying on the bed, which still seems to contain an arm, as if a hand were reaching under the blanket. Water rushes inside the bathroom.

Clara comes back into the room with her blouse unbuttoned, quickly puts on her coat and says, I feel sick, I threw up. Her purse is on the pillow. Her mouth is half open, her tongue white and dry, like a piece of bread in her mouth.

You're afraid, says Adina, you look like death. Clara is startled, her gaze is straight and cutting. She looks at Adina and sees a face that has gone somewhere far away. A face all twisted into separate parts, the cheeks off by themselves and the lips off by themselves, lifeless and eager at the same time. A face that's as empty from the side as it is from the front, like a picture with nothing on it.

Clara searches the empty face for a child who is walking alongside a woman and who is nevertheless all alone, because she's carrying Christmas trees from one house to the next. A child like the one in her belly, she thinks, as alone as a child that no one knows about.

Adina wants to be the hunter, thinks Clara.

Anyway you seem more afraid than I am, says Adina. Stop looking, don't look at the fox anymore.

Clara's eyes are skewed, with tiny red veins in the shadow of her nose. She looks absently at the picture on the wall, the clunky shoes in the grass, the soldier's uniform, the grass straw in Ilie's mouth. You better not tell Ilie, says Clara, he won't be able to stand it.

You're not saying anything

The stairwell has no window, the stairwell has no daylight. The stairwell has no electricity, the elevator is stuck between the upper floors. Pavel's lighter sparks but doesn't cast light. The key finds the keyhole. The door handle doesn't click and the door doesn't creak as it opens. Inside the apartment the door to the main room is open, letting a bright square of light into the front hall. Inside the room the sewing machine is humming.

Pavel takes off his shoes and tiptoes into the kitchen in stocking feet. Outside the kitchen window pant legs are fluttering in the wind. Pavel doesn't see the clothesline. The buckles on his briefcase are cold. He places a package of Jacobs coffee and a tub of breakfast margarine on top of the kitchen cupboard. He counts out twelve packs of cigarettes and sets them beside the coffee. He opens the refrigerator and puts the meat inside. Next to the refrigerator is an umbrella. He picks it up.

Pavel tiptoes toward the room. The little wheel on the sewing machine is turning, the belt moves, the thread creeps off the bobbin, Clara pumps her feet in a steady rhythm. Pavel stands in the doorway and pops open the umbrella. There's a ferocious storm outside, dear lady, he says, might I stay the night. Clara's eyes laugh, her mouth stays serious. Certainly, dear sir, please do come in and get out of those wet clothes. The umbrella drops to the floor and the sewing machine wheel stops in mid-stitch.

Clara's hand is in his underpants. Her hair cascades across his face. Oh sir, I see you're frozen quite stiff, says her mouth. Her thighs are hot and her belly deep and his penis thrusts.

The refrigerator resumes humming, the electricity has come back on. Clara sniffs at the package, switches on the light, the package crackles as her fingers open the coffee, she holds a coffee bean up to his birthmark, are you coming from work, she asks, the coffee grinder cuts off her voice. The flame licks at the pot, the water starts to bubble. She drops three spoonfuls of coffee into the water without wetting the spoon. The spoon handle clinks against the stove, could you ever do anything to Adina, she asks. The coffee rises and foams, Clara skims off some of the foam with the spoon. What do you mean, he asks. She lets a little foam into each of the two cups. What do you mean, he asks. The foam in the spoon is as bright as sand. Could you ever poison Adina, she asks, lifting the pot from the stove.

A black thread of coffee trickles into the foam. No, he says. The foam rises up to the cup handles. Because she's my friend, says Clara. He carries the cups to the table, outside the window the pants are fluttering in the wind. That's one reason, he says, picking up a sugar cube, what is she after anyway, doesn't she realize where she's living. She's not after anything, she simply says things because she's angry, says Clara. The sugar cube tears the layer of foam and sinks into the cup.

Whenever my father got angry, says Pavel, he just turned silent. You couldn't argue with him. He would go for days without saying a word. It made my mother furious. Once she dragged him away from the table and pressed his face against the mirror and shook him by the hair. Just take a look at yourself, she screamed, but he didn't even blink. As if his eyes went straight through the mirror without seeing his own reflection. His face became a stone. And when she let go of his hair his head sprang back. Then my father did look in the mirror and saw me standing there. In a very quiet voice he said, always pay attention to a person's tongue because every person carries red hot coals in his mouth. And one angry word can ruin more in one breath than two feet can trample over an entire lifetime. Pavel's spoon clinks against his cup.

You choose who you're going to pick on, says Clara, but they just say out loud what all of us think, including you. He stirs his coffee, the foam floats onto the rim. We're all victims, he says. His lighter clicks, he holds the flame for her, she pulls the ashtray from the edge of the table close to her hand. You ask what Adina's after, says Clara, what do you think she's after, she wants to live.

Clara rolls the cigarette in her hand. He sips the coffee, sees her eyes above the rim of the cup. What are you going to do with the person who finally shoots Ceaușescu, she asks. She swallows her breath without exhaling the smoke.

Pavel has a knot in his throat and coffee grounds on his tongue. That depends, he says. On what, she asks. He doesn't answer.

Clara stands by the window, sees the pants fluttering and the ball stuck in the fork of the tree, the green ball that had been hidden by the swaying foliage all summer long. And had remained wedged there for two bare winters because no child dared climb up the smooth trunk onto the thin branches.

What would happen then, Clara's mouth asks into the windowpane. He runs his fingers through her hair. Then I'll get divorced and we'll get married, he says. He can feel her temples pulsing in his hand. Besides, the man has cancer and doesn't have much longer to live, he says, digging deeper into her hair and pressing on her skull.

He'll outlive us all, says Clara. Pavel turns her head with his hands, he wants to see her face. He has cancer, I have that from a reliable source, says Pavel. But he can't turn her eyes away from the green ball.

You have to help Adina, she says. He reaches in his pants pocket, twists the cap off the perfume flask, sprinkles a couple of drops on the curve of her neck, what does it smell like, he says and drops the cap into her blouse. He places the open bottle on the table, the scent hangs in the kitchen, oppressively heavy on Clara's neck.

She tears her eyes away from the fork in the tree, from this dented green ball, from this mute summer game stuck in the branches.

It smells like secret police, says Clara.

He goes into the room and bumps into the open umbrella. He stands in the hall and puts on his shoes. Your key's on the bed, says Pavel, his fingers searching for the laces.

You can keep my key, says Clara, that way you won't need to have one made. His shoes pinch, they are narrow and hard. You have Adina's key as well, except she never gave you one.

Two places are set on the table. The two forks are touching each other but not the knives. And the tub of margarine has been scooped out in two corners, down to the plastic bottom. Some bread crumbs have fallen on the margarine, and a bit of crust is on Pavel's plate.

You're not saying anything, he says.

She opens the refrigerator and puts the margarine inside. The square of light falls on her feet. I'm going, he says. Her cheek is cold. The meat is packed in cellophane, the cellophane is coated with frost, like the gardens outside.

Pavel's feet are confused, but his hand is sure, it finds the door handle. He pulls the door shut with a bang.

The next morning Clara leaves the umbrella right where it was, still open. The umbrella comes from Pavel. Also the dress in the sewing machine. Also the needle stopped in mid-stitch. And the roses in the vase.

The green ball in the fork of the tree peers into the kitchen, the coffee water is boiling. The coffee comes from Pavel, the sugar cubes, the cigarette Clara is smoking, the sweater she is wearing, the pants, the panty hose. Also the earrings, the mascara, the lipstick. And last night's perfume.

The cold cigarette smoke leaves a sour taste on her tongue. Her cold breath flies into the air like smoke and tastes sour in her mouth. The dust on the streets lapping behind the trucks has a different smell than the dust of summer. And the clouds in the city have a different smell than they do in summer. Clara paces back and forth in front of the secret police building.

Two men come down the stairs, then one man, three men, a woman who pulls on a sheepskin jacket as she walks.

A calendar is stuck to the wall behind the guard's head. Spring, summer, fall, each past month has been crossed off, almost an entire year. The guard stands up to his stomach in the gatehouse window.

Clara feels her throat tighten, she lights a cigarette, have you been summoned, asks the guard, she doesn't put her lighter away and offers him the pack of cigarettes. He rests his left hand on the telephone and slowly pulls two cigarettes out with his right. One he sticks in his mouth, the other in the left breast pocket of his uniform. One for the mouth and one for the heart, he says. His lighter flickers, he looks at her, so who would you like to see, he asks, blowing the smoke up into his hair. She says: PAVEL MURGU. He dials a number with the hand holding the cigarette, who shall I say is calling, he asks. She says: CLARA. The cigarette sticks out of his breast pocket like a finger, Clara who, he asks, she says, Comrade MURGU will know.

The trucks rattle outside, it's cold and dreary and isn't snowing. The trees shake the dust onto the road, have you known the Comrade Colonel very long, asks the gatekeeper, she nods. I've never seen you here before, he says. He listens with his throat, with his chin in the receiver, the ash drops, yes yes he says. The cigarette has slipped all the way down into his breast pocket. You may wait for him in the café across the street, he says, the Comrade Colonel will be there in a quarter hour.

The waitress is wearing a white lace crown on the middle of her head. Her hair is gray, she hums a song as she passes between the smoke and the empty tables. The trucks hum through the windowpane, from above you can see what they're carrying, sacks and lumber. The waitress balances a tray with five glasses, five policemen are sitting at the table. Next to them are six men in suits and the woman in the sheepskin jacket.

The ceiling has a brown water stain and a light fixture with five arms, four empty sockets and one bulb. The bulb is burning but all it lights is the rising smoke. The woman in the sheepskin calls out MITZI, the waitress sets the empty tray on the table, and one of the men in suits says, seven Jamaica rums. A truck shakes the windowpane. The truck is carrying barrels and pipes. Who knows where they come from, thinks Clara, the barrels and pipes are covered with snow.

Sitting in the corner, next to the door, are two old men with stubbly, toothless faces. They are playing cards. One is wearing a verdigris ring. The cards are notched and worn thin, ace of clubs, says the man with the ring, but there are no clubs left on the card he pulls from his hand, only gray spots.

Comrade MURGU, says the man with the verdigris ring.

Pavel shakes his hand, how are you getting along with life, he asks. The man wearing the ring laughs with his black empty mouth, how about one more on you, Comrade MURGU, he says. Pavel nods, the laughing mouth calls out MITZI.

The other man sets his cards facedown on the table, once upon a time our MITZI was a great singer, he says. The waitress hums, two Jamaica rums, says the man with the ring. MITZI may be a daughter of the working class, says the other, but she really is an angel. Those were the days, our MITZI was young and famous throughout the city, down at the ŞARI-NENI, they had the best singers and down in the cellar they made the clearest brandy.

Pavel looks over to Clara, and Clara listens as she watches a truck outside drive through the winter dust. The truck is carrying sand and stones.

In those days educated people still drank with the poor folk, says the man with the verdigris ring. One time the professor took a burnt matchstick and drew a picture just for me illustrating the human soul, it was incredibly thin. And the royal notary only had eyes for our MITZI. She had a mouth like a rose, says the man with the verdigris ring, and a voice like a nightingale.

The other snickers with wilted lips. And breasts like white porcelain, he says, and her nipples were more beautiful than most other women's eyes.

The men in suits laugh, one of the policemen pulls off his cap and bangs it on the table, the woman in the sheepskin jacket strokes the curls around her collar, Pavel nods to her, claps the man next to her on the shoulder.

The waitress carries her tray, she does not hum as she walks. She is clearly moved, her face is soft, her eyes transfigured, she places two Jamaica rums on the cards in front of the toothless men, smiles and sighs and strokes the head of the one with the verdigris ring.

Pavel perches on the chair. I'm so happy, he says to Clara, let's have a drink, he looks at the stain on the ceiling. The waitress comes, two Jamaica rums, he says, and touches Clara's hand with a fingertip. We're pretty conspicuous here, he says, everyone's listening and everyone's watching.

Do you like it here, asks Clara. Pavel tugs on his tie, as much as you do in the factory, he says.

My head is dark

Adina comes home from school in the afternoon. She washes the chalk off her hands because it gnaws away her fingers. Two sunflower seeds are floating in the toilet bowl. She knows even before she can think it, the fox.

The second hind leg has been cut off and shoved against the fur as if it were still attached. Apart from that everything is the way it was, room, table, bed, kitchen, bread, sugar, flour. Blind air presses against the window outside, blind walls stare at one another. Adina asks herself how the room, the table, the bed can allow this to happen.

Adina sets her alarm clock for early in the morning, the hands revolve, the grass straw turns in Ilie's mouth. She's made up her mind to go see him.

The flashlight isn't enough to see by, but the circle in front of her shoes is just bright enough to make her avert her eyes. The figures at the streetcar are empty clothes pacing back and forth, with full bags even at this early hour.

The tracks squeal, the streetcar whooshes past the buildings. The bright windows slow down as they pass, the people waiting all know where the door will open when the car comes to a stop. Elbows push. Sleep rides along with the passengers, their winter sweat has a bitter odor. When the streetcar makes a turn the light blinks once or twice, it's yellow and weak and nonetheless jumps right in your face. Two reddish-brown chickens peek out of a woman's basket. They crane their necks and hold their beaks half-open as if searching for air. Their eyes are flat and reddish-brown like their feathers. But when they crane their necks, a pinhead shines inside the pupils.

One spring the seamstress from the outskirts of town bought ten chicks at the market. She didn't have a broody hen. I sit here and sew and they just grow on their own, she said. As long as they still had their down feathers she kept the chicks in the workshop, where they scampered around or sat on the scraps of fabric and warmed themselves. After they grew bigger they were out in the yard from dawn to dusk. But one chick always stayed in the workshop. It hopped over the scraps on just one leg, the other was crippled. It perched for hours watching the seamstress sew. When she got up it would hop after her. If there weren't any customers she would talk to it. The chicken had rusty red feathers and rusty red eyes. Since it ran around the least it grew the fastest and became fat the soonest. That chicken was the first one killed, before the summer had really settled in. The other chickens scrabbled around in the courtyard.

The seamstress talked about the crippled chicken for a whole summer. I had to kill it, she said, it was like a child.

The man on the platform has a large black mustache on his face, a large black velvet hat on his head, and a three-legged sheet-metal stove in front of his stomach. The woman next to him has a floral headscarf, a flowery skirt, and a one-elbow stove pipe under her arm. And the child next to her has a cap with a thick tassel on his head and a stove door in his hand.

Adina enters the compartment. An old man is sitting across from a mother and father, with their child between them all bundled up.

The night begins to tatter. Adina looks at the viaduct above the tracks, and the stairs leading up to it. Large shapes in dark clothes climb the stairs, the ones already on the viaduct seem small, as if they were walking around heaven, as if anyone who made it there got shrunk by half, like a child shriveled with age, before the workday has even begun.

The stairs on the other side of the viaduct lead down to the factory gate. Even with the trains running through your ears you can still hear the factory.

Sleep, says the mother, the child leans against her shoulder. The housing blocks loom in the dark. Behind them, at the edge of the city, is the city prison, the watchtowers ride past the window, with an identical soldier frozen inside each one. Another Ilie, thinks Adina, one trusted by the night, by the cold, by authority and power and by his weapon, even when he's all alone.

For a year Ilie had to travel to Bucharest every month on duty, always taking this same route out of town, past the prison. The cells are located in back, by the prison yard. People who don't have family or friends locked up don't see the cells, Ilie said back then, but those who do have someone there know where to look. For a few hundred meters along this stretch, he said, the faces inside the compartment separate. And it's obvious which eyes know where to look.

The trick is to stay asleep, then you won't feel anything, the father tells the child. The child nods. The woman with the reddish-brown chicks walks past the compartment.

I always used to sleep in the train, says the old man, and in the streetcar too. Every morning I'd ride into town from our village and every evening I'd ride back. For twenty-seven years I had to be on the platform at five in the morning. I knew the way like I know the Lord's Prayer. Once I bet someone a sheep that I could make it to the station with my eyes closed, and I won that sheep. I found the way blindfolded, and in the middle of winter with ice and snow on top of that. And it's a long way, too, more than three thousand steps. Back then, he says, I knew every crack in the earth, I knew where there was a hump and where there was a hole. And I knew three streets ahead of time where a dog was going to bark and where a rooster would crow. And if the rooster didn't crow on Monday I knew it had been killed on Sunday. I always fell asleep at work, the man said, I was a tailor and I could even sleep with a needle in my mouth.

I want an apple, says the child, and the mother says, sleep now, and the father says, oh give him an apple.

But now I'm old, says the man, and I can't sleep anymore, not even in my bed. That doesn't matter, he says, doesn't matter at all.

The child bites into the apple, chews slowly and bores his

finger into the hole. Is it good, asks the mother and the child says, it's cold.

On Mondays during the winter, Adina's father would bring a bag full of little apples back from the slaughterhouse. They were so cold that their skins fogged up white the way eyeglasses do. Adina would eat one right away. The first bite hurt, the flesh was so cold it uncoiled into her temples before she could swallow it. And with the second piece the cold filled her whole head. That bite didn't hurt anymore because her brain was already frozen.

After Adina had eaten the cold apple she took three more into the yard and let them freeze overnight. She set them on a rock, a hand's width apart, so the dark frost could gnaw all around the peel. In the morning she thawed them in the kitchen. Then they were soft and brown. Frozen apples were Adina's favorite.

The child's father has stepped out of the compartment and has been standing a long time in the corridor with the bare field in his forehead. He has spotted three deer, each time he called to the sleeping mother, and each time she shifted her head and the child but didn't get up.

Now the other passengers are crowding into the corridor, Adina as well, along with a round woman wearing a fox collar with tied paws, and the thin old man who won a bet and a sheep.

The Danube is riding along with the train, the passengers can see the far bank and the roads on the other side, thin as a thread, and moving cars and forests. Not a single shoe shuffles in the corridor, no one moves, no one speaks. The old man's eyes, too, widen and press away his wrinkles. The father catches his breath, a forbidden sigh. Then he closes his mouth, look, Yugoslavia, he calls into the compartment. But the mother stays in her seat. Her brother swam across six years ago, he says, now he's in Vienna. He squints, trying to make out individual waves in the glare, do you have children, he asks. Adina says, no.

The waiting room has no bench, just a cold cast-iron stove. The cracked concrete floor is strewn with light green spittle and sunflower seeds. Above the stove is a wall newspaper with the dictator's portrait appearing three times, the black inside the eye is as big as the button on Adina's coat. It shines. And the spit on the floor shines.

Everything that shines also sees.

There's a bench outside the station, Ilie wrote her in the summer, the bus stop is next to that. The bus is only for officers riding out to their unit from the small town. Still, now and then the driver will give the soldiers a lift, but he prefers to take young women.

Five officers are sitting in the bus. They wear green caps with gray fur earflaps bound with green ties. The officers' ears are visible below the flaps, rimmed red from the burning frost. The backs of their heads are shaven.

The driver is wearing a hat, and underneath his coat he's wearing a suit. White cuffs with dark streaks of dirt and thick blue buttons stick out of his coat sleeves. A signet ring gleams on his left hand. Three officers climb in.

Where to, the driver asks. Adina hoists her bag onto the step, to the unit, she says. As he bends over, his blue scarf drops over his hand. He carries her bag into the aisle, our army is always in need of beautiful women, he says. The officers break out in a squall of laughter.

Adina takes the first seat, next to an officer with white-haired temples. The smell of damp winter clothes fills the air. Who is the young lady hoping to visit, asks a voice from the back, and Adina turns her head and sees a gold tooth behind the empty seats. Her black coat is lost in all the green coats. A soldier, she says. Outside the window a factory spews pipes and fencing into an open field. The driver raises his hand and says, we have a lot of those, when we get there the young lady can pick whichever one she wants.

The corn turns away from the window, broken, forgotten in the frost, why just one, says the man with the gold tooth, this country has more than enough to spare. The laughter bursts ahead into a section of forest that is black and bare.

What's your soldier's name, asks the officer next to Adina, his temples are made of paper, his eyes look at her hands, his coat makes his eyeballs shimmer green. She says, his name is Dolga. Crows fly over the field, and the officer says, we have two of those, and the man with the gold tooth laughs so loud that his left earflap comes untied and drops onto his epaulette. He takes off his cap, his hair is matted down, his temples shaven. He reties the earflaps, the strings are short, his fingers are fat, he closes his lips over his gold tooth, the bow gets as small as two fingertips, he sets his cap back on his head.

What's his first name, asks the officer next to Adina, she draws her fingers up inside her coat sleeve and says, Ilie.

Outside is a ditch overgrown with thin reeds, what does the young lady do for a living, asks the officer next to Adina, twisting his coat button. Behind the bend Adina sees the poplar lane that Ilie described, and a brick wall and the barracks. Teacher, she says.

Ilie wrote that everything is flat, that when you're outside you sit or lie in nothingness, and even though the shortest plants can block your view you can stand up and still be looking nowhere.

From the bus she sees the wind silently tearing at the tree rows. In that case do you know *The Last Night of Love, the First Night of War* says an officer behind the driver, a book like life itself, young lady, a beautiful book.

They all have bare necks, bare temples, Adina thinks, they've been shorn like that for years, none of them is young. But at some point they will laugh and in the middle of their laughter, in the middle of the squall, they will look at one another and see that their stamped-down sacks of cut hair are full and weigh as much as they do.

Ilie's hands are jittery, his fingernails dirty and torn. For an hour I had the compartment all to myself, says Adina, there was no sun to be seen, but there were shadows everywhere, then I fell asleep.

I dreamed, says Adina, that a fox was crossing an empty field that had just been plowed. As it moved it stooped down and swallowed some earth. It ate and ate and got fatter and fatter.

Next to the door is a blackboard, and a picture showing a tank at the edge of the forest. Sitting on the tank is a group of soldiers, one of the soldiers is Ilie. The officers are standing in the grass.

You have it good, says Ilie, you can still feel fear, my head is dark, I haven't had any dreams for a long time. Above and below the tank are portraits of the dictator, the black inside the eye. Here you have to forget yourself day after day, says Ilie, the only thing I remember about me is that I always think of you. The unit's honors are on display beside the black inside the eye.

Ilie points to the tank. In October, he says, we took the tank out into open terrain. He kisses Adina's fingers, what terrain, she asks, it's all flat here. You have to drive out a ways, he says, there's a hill back there by the forest. To keep the tank from slipping when we went uphill we had to get out and throw rocks under the track from behind and then on the way down we had to throw rocks from in front. Once the tank was down by the edge of the forest we all lay down in the grass. We spent the whole day like that. And in the evening we marched back to the barrack on foot.

His hands are rough, he laughs and swallows his voice, that tank's still out there by the forest, he says. You know, if the Russians had waited for us they would never have made it to Prague. Now come on and I'll show you the yard.

Ilie stops in front of a pile of wet sandbags, they make us drag those from the wall to the fence, the fence to the road, and from the road back to the wall, he says. His footsteps clatter, he points at his clunky boots. As soon as it's summer I won't be needing these anymore. And the only soft road I know around here is the Danube.

A soldier walks by carrying a steaming bucket. Adina pulls her coat in close and wraps her arms around herself. So then the summer after that your bones will be lying out in the wheat. Ilie's face is straining ahead. The poplar lane is shrinking, crawling into the earth because it will soon be dark. But you'll come with me, he says. His throat is long, his neck and temples shaven bare. He bows in her direction and she shakes her head.

You'll be flying around in heaven, says Adina, an angel with a bullet wound. Then she looks at the ground. Or else you'll be down on the pavement, driving a street sweeper in Vienna. And you'll still be here, says Ilie, waiting for them to cut up the rest of your fox, and then what.

The fox on the table

The alarm ticks and ticks. Three a.m.

Maybe the fox paws have reattached themselves during the night, Adina thinks. She sticks her foot out of the bed and slides the hind legs away from the fur. The tail gives her toes a fright, it's still so soft and bushy and not shriveled up despite having been cut off.

Adina picks up the two legs and tail and takes them to the kitchen. She sets them on the table and fits them together so it looks like the fox is crawling right through the tabletop, that while its tail and hind legs support it from the top, the rest is rummaging around below.

The moon inside the kitchen window is so bloated it can't stay there. By six a.m. it has been gnawed by the morning and its face is bleary-eyed. The early buses go whooshing by, or perhaps that's the moon trying to leave the city and its jagged edge is getting caught on the border of the night. Dogs yelp as if the darkness had been a large sheltering pelt and the deserted streets an untroubled brain. As if the dogs of the night were afraid of the daylight, when people are out and about, and when the hunger that seeks encounters the hunger that strays. When yawn meets yawn and speech meets bark with the same breath inside the mouth.

Adina's stockings smell of winter sweat, they jerk like the train as she tugs them on over her bare legs. Then she puts her coat on over her nightgown—and with it all the little black coats from the viaduct and the big green coats from the bus. The little train station is still there in the buttons on her coat and so is the black inside the eye. Her coat pocket still contains her flashlight and some money from the trip. Her keys are on the kitchen table. The filth from the barracks yard still clings to her soles. Adina slips into her shoes.

The flashlight circle stumbles, the curbstone is poorly rounded. A cat leaps out of the garbage bin, leaving a sound of broken glass, its paws are white.

The parking lot is empty, the stadium keeps its earthen wall in the dark, the sky overhead turns gray. From the factory in back of the stadium comes the sound of clanging iron. The smokestack isn't visible, only the yellow smoke. The streetcar squeals around the corner. Some windows are lit and awake, others are dark and asleep.

Morning comes later to the quiet streets of power. The windows stay dark, the lanterns hanging from their ornate lampposts illuminate the stone angels and lions, their circles of light are private property, they do not belong to those passing through, to those who themselves do not belong in these streets.

The poplars are knives, they hide their blades, and sleep while standing. Over at the café the white iron chairs have been cleared and stored, winter doesn't need a chair, winter doesn't sit, it stamps around the river and lurks under the bridges. The water doesn't shine and doesn't see, it leaves the poplars alone.

Early in the evening the fishermen go to bed and early in the morning they stand outside the stores. In the afternoon they meet in the smoky café and drink and talk until the water starts to shine again. Morning fog hides the clock in the cathedral bell tower when it strikes seven, but the tops of the acacias are already awake. Locks are now unlocked, latches shoved aside, shop doors opened. Gray light peels the bark off the acacia twigs, and at the edge of the park thorns peek out of every branch, but the trunks below don't notice.

Adina is the first customer in the store. The cashier puts a windbreaker on over her light blue smock. Her fur cap swallows her eyebrows. Adina picks up a basket. The jars of marmalade are arranged in rows. They are all the same height, have the same dust, the same bulging glass and the same tin lids and labels. If an officer were to walk by, Adina thinks, they would salute. They are distinguished only by the amount of rust on the lids and the drops that have leaked out and stick to the labels.

Adina places a bottle of brandy in her basket. The cashier is drinking coffee that sends steam into her face. No alcohol before ten, she says, then takes one short and one long slurp of coffee and wipes the drops off her chin. She raises her eyes halfway into her cap and sets down her coffee cup. She reaches into the basket, the scuffed red nail polish makes her fingers look as though they were sprouting new tips. She moves the bottle next to the register.

Adina lays a bill next to the coffee cup. I've never been drunk in my life, she says quietly, it's seven in the morning, and I've never been drunk, and the day is just around the corner. It's seven in the morning, just like it's been seven in the morning every other day, and every day was just around the corner, and I've never been drunk before in my life. Her voice falls apart, her cheeks are flushed and wet, it's seven in the morning, here's my brandy and here's my money and a day around the corner and I've never been drunk, and I don't want to wait any longer, I want to get drunk right this minute and not wait till ten. The cashier presses the money back into Adina's hand, that's what a lot of people want, she says.

A man wearing a light blue smock takes Adina by the shoulders and shoves her to the door, chasing her out with the words law and brandy and police. Her shoes drag, the dried dirt from the barracks flakes off in little pieces and the wet dirt from the park breaks off in big clumps. Her nightgown is sticking out a couple inches under her coat. The cashier holds the door open. Who do you think you are, Adina screams, don't touch me, you hear, get your hands off me.

Adina rings three times. The door to the apartment opens, a glaring square of light blinds her face. She steps through the entry hall carrying a bare branch. Go into the kitchen, says Paul, Anna's still asleep in the other room. Adina nods once and twice and three times, he follows her and notices her nightgown sticking out under her coat. Adina hands him the bare branch and laughs, explodes with laughter, these are going to be lilacs, she says. She sits at the kitchen table, in front of a cup splattered with coffee that's sitting next to a key. Adina looks at the wall clock, lays a bill on the table and clutches her face. Here are my eyes, she says, here is my forehead and here is my mouth. She unbuttons her coat. And this is my nightgown, she says. And that's a wall clock, and a key on the table, and outside a day is just around the corner, and I'm not crazy, it's eight in the morning, it's eight in the morning every day, I want to get drunk right this minute and not wait till ten. She pushes the coffee cup to the edge of the table.

Paul stuffs the money into her coat pocket, sets a glass and then a bottle in front of her. He pours some brandy and presses the glass into her hand. She doesn't drink, she doesn't cry, her eyes water and her mouth is mute. He holds her head in his hands. Anna stands in the doorway, dressed but unshowered and uncombed. She picks up the key, puts on her shoes, tiptoes through the hall. The door closes with a bang.

You can stay, says Paul. I have to go to work. The door closes with a bang.

There in the hall are Adina's shoes. And there in the room is her coat draped over the chair, her stockings on the floor. The bare branch that's going to be lilacs is in a vase beside the bed. The bed is still warm from Anna.

The hand kiss

Adina pulls her stockings over her legs, but her legs aren't really inside the stockings. She puts on her coat, but her arms are not really in the coat. Her nightgown though is sticking out from underneath. She hikes it up so it isn't showing. Key, money, and flashlight are stashed inside her coat pocket. The sun is lying on the kitchen table, under the table is dirt from her shoes, the clock is ticking on the wall and listening to itself. It's almost noon. Adina slips into her shoes, her toes aren't really in the shoes, they're in the clock as she tiptoes out of the kitchen before both hands meet at the top where it is noon. The door opens and closes.

Adina's breath keeps just ahead of her as she walks, she clutches at it with her hand but it eludes her grasp. An old woman with a cane and a cloth sack is leaning against a garbage bin by the side of the road. Her sack is half full. Her cane has a nail on the bottom. The woman thrusts her head and her cane inside the garbage bin and spears dry bread with the nail.

The corner of the building is one big window. Through the glass Adina sees a man covered with a white cloth. The man is young and thin, his sack of hair won't be heavy when he dies, Adina thinks, no heavier than the sack full of speared bread. Scissors open and close, snippets of hair fall onto the cloth. The barber cuts, the barber talks. The barber is drawing out the time, extending it past the winter, just like Adina is drawing out the way home, because the fox is rummaging under the table, because a tree is standing right here in the middle of the asphalt, in front of the windowpane where hair is being cut, and because the tree itself is bare.

The trolleybus bends its black accordion. The bellows open and close. The horns overhead search out the way, the driver chews on an apple. A man jumps on before the steps fold out. His pant legs flutter, his shoes shine. He's wearing a windbreaker. The accordion squeals, tree trunks drift through the windowpane, coats pass slowly, and the traffic squeezes upward into the glass. The only thing the bus takes with it, at least for a little while, is a coffin that's lashed to the top of a red car—the road keeps the tree trunks at a distance as the coffin slides from one windowpane to the next. Some housing blocks ride by, fronted by a sidewalk that quickly turns into a wall. The coffin passes through the last window, and the man in the windbreaker watches it drift behind. Adina moves to the back of the bus. When the door opens, the man in the windbreaker pinches Adina's bottom. She stands on the stairs, pushes him away, she stumbles off, the door closes, dust flies.

The face of the man drives on. He shows her his fist in the window, then opens his fingers and blows her a kiss.

The fox is no longer rummaging underneath the table. The full fur is lying on the floor in front of the wardrobe. Adina sets her keys down on the table. She stands inside the room, but the room is only there for itself. The hind legs and tail have been shoved so close against the pelt that the cuts are invisible. Adina slides the left hind leg away with the tip of her shoe, then the right hind leg, then the tail. The right foreleg is still attached and pulls the stomach and the head along. The left foreleg leaves stomach and head where they lie. It has been cut off as well. The bed is unmade.

The kitchen, the apples, the bread.

Adina stands in the bathtub, and the bath is only there for itself. A cigarette butt is floating in the toilet bowl. It has been lying in the water for hours, swollen to bursting. Adina places the money and the flashlight on the table. She takes off her coat and stockings. She climbs into bed. Her toes are cold, her nightgown, the bed is cold. Her eyes are cold. She hears her heart beating on the pillow. She sees the table, the money, the flashlight, the chair, they are spinning inside her eyes. The alarm ticks and ticks until the light at the window disappears.

Something rings, not the alarm. Adina finds her toes and the floor next to the bed. She turns on the light, opens the door. A bright square falls into the stairwell, she laughs and holds out her cheek. Paul's mouth is cold. He is holding a bare branch, these are going to be lilacs, he says. She takes the branch in her hand and points a finger at the fox. Paul lifts each cut-off leg one at a time. As of today that makes three, she says, along with the tail. She looks at him and pulls the scarf off his neck. The back of his neck is shaved. I was at the barber's, he says.

She lays his scarf on the bed. In every room I've lived in, that fox was always in front of the wardrobe, even in the dormitory, where space was so cramped, she says, since there were four of us in one room. There was a cat in that dormitory who used to come up the front stairs and wander through all the rooms to the end of the hall. He was fat and nearly blind and no longer caught mice, but he would sniff out every bit of bacon and eat it. That cat never set foot in our room: he could smell the fox.

She holds the bare branch in her mouth. Don't make such a face, he says, or there won't be any lilacs. She goes into the kitchen, the vase has a brown ring from the last bunch of chrysanthemums. I saw Clara in the hospital yesterday, he says, while Adina sniffs at the branch, she was waiting where they do abortions. The faucet squeals, he stands in the door to the kitchen, there are bubbles on the water, she fills the vase up to the brown ring. She carries it past him back into the room and he follows.

One paw left, says Paul, that fox could drive a person insane. He places the branch in the water and sits down next to her. You're standing here right between the bed and the chair and suddenly you're in the middle of the woods, that fox is so close there's no need for any binoculars. The bare branch casts a bare shadow on his cheek. Incidentally, he says, this morning the gatekeeper got hold of the binoculars. But he wasn't looking at the woods out in back, he was watching the front entrance. He didn't even bother to lower them when I was standing right next to him, he just turned toward me and said, Sir, I'm looking at your eye and it's as big as a door. The bare shadow on Paul's face looks like a wrinkle. Then a man came, Paul went on, and gave the gatekeeper some money, since it wasn't a visiting day, and the gatekeeper let the man look through the binoculars, while I took off my coat and grabbed my white jacket. Paul touches Adina's fingertips with his own. How do you tell a man, he asks, who slips the porter money so he can go upstairs and take a mesh bag with a fresh loaf of bread that his wife died during the night because the electricity went out. He pulls Adina closer. You walk slowly, he says, because you can smell the fresh-baked bread. Adina feels his chin moving close to her head, sees snippets of hair lying in his ear. And you hope for his sake that when he looked through the binoculars they somehow had enough power to take away the fear for one whole day. She pulls her knees up inside her nightgown and rests her feet on his knee. But you hope in vain, he says, because you can tell by the man's steps that in a few minutes he's going to lose his mind.

Adina covers her face with one hand. Looking through her fingers she can see how light the twigs are, and how dark the branch is in the water.

Paul flicks the flashlight on and off. He picks the bill up off the table, this morning you wanted to give that to me, he says, smoothing it out with his hand. There's a face on the bill, dirty, crumpled and soft. Paul takes the longest twig and drills a hole in the face, then skewers the bill on the bare branch. One more paw, he says, and then.

The lost shovel

The left knee lifts, the right knee falls. The grass is trampled, the ground is soft. The muck skids off underfoot, the clunky boots chafe against the ankles. The laces are made of mud, twice torn and twice knotted between morning and noon. The socks are wet. The grime on the hands dries in the wind. The cap has fallen into the dirt.

The cigarette gets grimier from hand to hand, the smoking is interrupted by orders—one cigarette lit four times and put out three times between morning and noon while thin flights of smoke pass from mouth to mouth. The last man flings away the butt, still glowing.

At neck height the trench is deep enough. The light over the grass is as low as the tank in the forest, as the forehead over the eyes. And the day gets pulled into the ground somewhere between the forest and the hill.

It's evening, the soldiers watch from the corners of their eyes, the officer with the gold tooth gives an order and steps out to piss, he walks past the tank and then into the wood, three trees deep. The soldiers stop digging, they listen in silence for the officer's stream to hit the ground. But the branches crack, and the crows squawk as they fly to their roosts. The crows feel the fog slowly draping the trees. Maybe they sense the snow up in the flat ridge, the snow of the days ahead. Snow that is coarse and dry and stays put. Snow so white that their black beaks are always open and freezing because they can't find anything to eat except frozen corn.

The men don't hear the officer's stream hitting the ground.

The officer buttons his pants, pulls his cap down lower on his head, his scarf tighter around his neck. He picks up a withered branch and scrapes the dirt off his boots.

Fall in, count off, every voice is tired in its own way, every breath from every mouth is its own steamy animal. Two ranks, the tall and the short.

Right shoulder, shovels, shouts the officer. He inspects the ranks. DOLGA where is your shovel. Ilie raises his hand to his cap, clicks one shoe against the other, Comrade Officer Sir, my shovel has disappeared. The officer raises his forefinger, his gold tooth is brighter than his face, find it, he says, or you're not coming back to the unit. Right face, march, left right. The soldiers march up the hill alongside the tracks left by the tank. The hilltop swallows them from below, the sky from above.

Ilie no longer hears their lockstep, he searches the trench as they march alongside, the trench is darker than the ground. His hands ache from the shovel because it's no longer pressing against them, because they are no longer digging, because his calluses are softening into skin and they burn. His shoes find nothing but grass and dirt, his eyes nothing but the hill. The hill has moved into the night, and the forest is a dark corner without trees.

Behind that hill, thinks Ilie, is the flat plain. Perhaps at night it's made of water, of smooth, level water, so that he might make his escape. He would be black like the riverbank and the place where he jumped wouldn't see him and the water would carry him away. If I swim for a long time, he thinks, my eyes will get used to the night, they can lead me across many things, and once I have crossed everything there is to cross my hands will touch a different riverbank, a different country. But first I'll have to take off these clunky boots, he thinks, before I get to the top of the hill. I'll have to get rid of them before I jump, I can't lose time untying laces on the riverbank. And when tomorrow comes, just as early and just as dreary as today did, to the sound of a command and a gold tooth that's been awake for hours, tomorrow when the column follows the tank tracks up the hill, the boots will be there, and the trees will once again be in the forest and so will the crows.

Meanwhile in a mailbox far away is a letter for Adina. Inside the letter is a picture of him, with a weak smile and no grass straw in his mouth.

By the time the column reaches the hilltop Ilie is afraid of stepping out of his own soles. The plain is black, but the ground isn't made of water. He trudges alongside the tank ruts and is afraid of turning around to face himself. The trench has witnessed everything, and tomorrow the officer with the gold tooth will know, and that is treason. The officer's mouth will scream, his tooth will glow. And the hilltop will stand there mute and no longer remember that it spent the night inside Ilie's forehead, and that it was responsible for driving his see-through skull to thoughts of escape, all out of fear.

Now every step bores a hole in the stomach, every breath sticks a stone in the throat. Broken corn leaves scratch behind the knees, the grass comes up to the naked buttocks. Ilie has to take a shit. He raises his head and pushes. He tears a leaf off the stalk, a narrow, long corn leaf. The corn leaf breaks, his fingers stink. The cornfield stinks, and so does the forest. And the night and the moon that isn't there stink as well.

Ilie sobs and curses, mother of all soldiers and officers and tanks and trenches. And he curses, invoking the gods and everything the world has ever borne.

His curses are cold. They are not for eating and not for sleeping. Only for blundering about and freezing, they climb up between the cornstalks and choke on themselves. They are for churning up and laying down flat, an instant of rage and a long time keeping still.

Once a curse is lifted, it never existed.

I can't stand looking at the water when it's so cold out

I know what I know, Clara says out loud, the streetcar whooshes close to the barrier, Ilie is sensitive, she says. The bridge shudders, the trees push into the park. I knew he wouldn't be able to withstand the fox, she says quietly, sinking her red fingernails into her hair, and I also know he won't try to escape. The wind fans her hair out over her forehead. You don't know that, says Adina, how can you know that. She sees Clara's cheek, the sharp black corners of her eyes.

Without the fishermen the river is just a stripe of water in the city, with its smelly, lazy gullet lurking midway between the reflection and the river bottom.

Clara's shoes clatter on the pavement. Adina stops but Clara doesn't notice and takes another three steps, walking on the middle of the paving stones. Then she turns around and says to Adina, come on, I can't stand looking at the water when it's so cold out. Her hair is dark like the grassy weeds in the river. It's the kind of cold that makes you naked, says Adina. Clara tugs Adina's arm, I feel dizzy, she says. Then she takes a few steps down the footpath, away from the bank. Adina tosses a dried leaf into the water. But it's not the river that's making you nauseous, is it, she says. She watches the leaf get so wet and heavy the little waves can no longer move it along. Paul saw you in the hospital, she says.

I know, says Clara, and I knew he'd tell you all about it, too. She sinks her red fingernails into her pocket and pushes her coat out to form a belly. I was pregnant, she says. The curved white wrists resurface, but not the fingernails. How did you manage an abortion, Adina asks. A wet leaf sticks to Clara's thin heel, Pavel knows the doctor, she says.

The grass in the park is frozen and matted down, it lies in thick empty clumps along the path. Even without their leaves the branches overhead are listening in.

Clara picks up a grass straw, she doesn't have to pull, it's just lying there, unattached. The straw has snapped in the middle and doesn't stay upright between her fingers. Adina turns around, but the cracking sound she hears is only a twig breaking under her shoe and not some stranger's footstep. Is he a doctor, asks Adina, and Clara says, he's a lawyer. Adina turns around, but the noise is only an acorn falling on the path and not some stranger's footstep. Why didn't you tell me, asks Adina. Clara pitches the grass straw, it's too light to fly and lands on her shoe. Because he's married, she says. They hear steps on the path and sand chafing against the stones, a woman walks by wheeling a bicycle with a sack slung across the handlebars. Why are you hiding him from me, asks Adina. Because he's married, says Clara. The woman looks back. We rarely see each other, says Clara. How long have you known him, asks Adina.

Nine soldiers and one officer are standing outside the cinema. The officer hands out tickets. The soldiers compare seats and rows. The poster shows a laughing soldier and a closed railroad gate stretching from one cheek to the other. A blue sky is over the soldier's cap, and under his face is the title of the film: THEY SHALL NOT PASS.

Clara elbows Adina and points her chin at the soldiers, look at them, the way they're standing there, she says. Adina's eyes stray into the dark green yews, I see them, she said, Ilie isn't with them.

A voice greets, the dwarf on his tall, half-brick shoes.

Clara smiles. It's cold here in town, says the dwarf. Clara nods. His head is too large, his hair is thick and looks so bright against the dark green yews, like the frozen matted grass in the park. It's already cooled down, says the dwarf, it was still warm when I bought it. He is carrying a loaf of bread under his arm.

There was a time and is no more

An old man is using a handcart to haul a propane tank. Hanging from the valve cap is a bag with a loaf of bread. The cart has a broom handle for a shaft and wheels taken from a child's tricycle. The wheels are narrow and get stuck in the cracks between the paving stones. For a few steps the man has the gait of a scrawny horse. The cap rattles. The man stops and the broom handle clatters onto the pavement. The man sits on the tank and tears off a piece of bread. As he chews he looks at the poplars, first down at the trunks and then up at the branches.

Shoes thud in the back of her head, steps clatter in the back of her neck. Adina turns around and sees a man's hands popping sunflower seeds into his mouth, his shoes shine, his pant legs flutter, his windbreaker scrunches. Now she feels the clatter on her cheek. It's the man from the bus where the moving coffin drifted from one window to the next. You'll do for me, he says, and spits a sunflower seed onto the stone, I'm sure you're good in bed. She sees a bench, but there's an empty bottle on the seat. I bet you're a really good screw, he says, the next bench has bare nails sticking out where there used to be a wooden slat. Get lost, she says, and sits down in the middle of the third empty bench. He spits a sunflower seed onto the bench, she leans back. He sits down. There are plenty of other benches, she says and moves to the end. Now he leans back and looks her in the face. She sits up, get lost or I'll scream, she says. He stands and says, that doesn't matter, doesn't matter at all. He laughs to himself, then opens his pants and holds out his penis. In that case I'll be on my way, he says, as he pisses into the river. She gets up, so disgusted that her tongue rises to her eyes and she doesn't see the paving stones as she starts walking. She feels cold water flowing into her ears and filling her head. He shakes the drops from his penis. I'll pay you, he calls after her, I'll give you a hundred lei, I'll piss in your mouth.

Adina stands on the bridge, the man walks slowly in the other direction, back the way he came. His pant legs flutter, his legs are thin. As he walks his hand keeps coming up to his face, he's still eating sunflower seeds. His back is narrow.

He walks like a quiet man.

How does the one go about the little Romanian who arrives in hell, Abi says to Paul and Adina. They are sitting in the café. That's what he asked me when he came to my office, says Abi. I told him I had no idea. And yet three weeks ago you knew it well enough to tell it, he said. Then he said, but anyone can see you really believe little ones go to heaven, not hell, and that is a contradiction. I opened my desk drawer because I have a cold and wanted to get my handkerchief and he told me to close the drawer. I asked why and he said there might be something there he shouldn't see. I said it's just a desk drawer and he said that after four and a half years every drawer becomes an intimate place. I laughed and said I didn't realize he was so tactful. Then he said he was a lawyer by profession and well bred. So, what does the little Romanian see when he gets to hell, he asked. Then he told the whole joke himself: A little Romanian dies and goes to hell, there's a lot of pushing and shoving and everybody's up to their neck in boiling mud. The devil sends the little Romanian off to the last empty space in the corner, and the man goes there and sinks up to his chin. From there he catches sight of a man close to the devil's throne who's also standing in boiling mud but only up to his knees. The little Romanian cranes his neck and recognizes Ceaușescu. Where's the justice in that, he asks the devil, that man has a lot more to atone for than I do. You're right, says the devil, but he's standing on top of his wife.

He laughed and laughed, then he realized he was laughing and his face got all sharp, he pulled in his shoulders and his birthmark twitched on his jugular vein. He hated me because he couldn't help laughing. He moved his hands quickly, like a knife and fork, he took a piece of paper out of his briefcase and placed a pen on the table. Write, he said. I picked up the pen and he looked out the window at the factory yard and dictated, I, and I asked, ME or YOU, and he said, write I and then your name. My name should be enough, I said, after all that's who I am. Then he shouted at me, write what I tell you, and then he realized he was shouting so he put his hand to his chin and clasped the corners of his mouth with his thumb and forefinger and said quietly, write I and then write your name. I did that. Then he said, WILL TELL NO PERSON, NO MATTER HOW CLOSE, OF MY COLLABORATION WITH. I put down the pen and said, I can't write that. He asked why, and I said, I can't live with that. I see, he said, his jaw was clenched so hard his temple pulsed but his voice stayed completely calm. I stood up and stepped away from the table, I went to the window, looked out into the yard, and said, I don't wish to be bothered here at work ever again. Well, he said, I imagined you preferred that to being interrupted during your free time. He stuck the pen in his jacket and crumpled up the paper and stashed it in his briefcase. He opened the briefcase all the way and I saw a picture inside. All I could really make out was a wall, but that wall looked very familiar. You think that we're chasing after you, he said, but you'll see, you'll end up coming to us all on your own. He shut the briefcase and then the door. After he was gone I saw my father at this wall, with sunken cheeks and large ears. It was the last picture my mother ever received from my father.

What was this man's name, asks Adina, and Paul says, MURGU, and Abi says PAVEL MURGU. How old, asks Adina, and Paul says, thirty-five, forty-five. He's younger than forty-five, says Abi.

The café is dark, the curtains on the wall of windows are dark red, the tablecloths are dark red and swallow what little light there is. All the coats and caps are black. The lightbulbs glow only for themselves, the smoke is brighter than they are and lingers like sleep lulled by voices. Outside, in the spaces between the curtains, evening settles along the river and on the empty paving stones. The poplar trunks stand for themselves on their own feet, the wind along the river path whirls for itself, herding the dried leaves together and shooing them away again. The fishermen sit in the café, drinking their fill. They drink until they can no longer distinguish the evening from the booze in their heads. Now and then, when their eyes happen to see through the window, a leaf drops from the sky. And they know it comes from far away, because the poplars by the water are already as bare as fishing rods. The fishermen don't trust the bare poplars. In the winter, say the fishermen, the bare poplars consume all happiness, even when the fishermen are drinking.

Who did you tell the joke to, asks Paul. If only I could remember, says Abi.

The fisherman afraid of melons balances a bottle of brandy on his head. The bottle is half full. He stretches his arms out like wings and walks once around the table without dropping the bottle.

The day after the concert MURGU read me a written statement, says Paul, saying that Face without Face refers to Ceaușescu. He claimed the explanation came from you, I didn't believe him. Then he showed me the actual paper, which had your handwriting. Abi looks at Paul. There was a man screaming in the room next door, he says, I could hear the blows. He told me what to write and I wrote out everything he said. Those screams were from a recording, Paul says and looks at Adina, who is staring out between the two faces into emptiness. And inside that emptiness Abi's face has sunken cheeks and large ears. That couldn't have been a recording, says Abi, I don't believe it. They kept me there until after midnight, he says. Afterward I went down the stairs and looked inside the guardhouse. There was a hand-sized mirror propped against the telephone, and next to it was an ashtray with water and a shaving brush. The guard had white lather on his face and was holding a razor. I couldn't believe my eyes. I looked for the birthmark on his neck. Only when I was standing right next to him and he took the razor off his cheek and yelled at me to close the door because I was letting in a draft did I realize it was just a guard shaving. By then the street was completely empty, says Abi, it was pitch-dark. But I kept seeing the white lather in front of my feet. Then the streetcar pulled up with just one car, the windows were bright but all empty except for the conductor. I saw white lather on his face too. I couldn't bring myself to get in.

The fisherman afraid of melons raises the bottle to his mouth, he doesn't drink, just closes his eyes, kisses the mouth of the bottle, and hums a song. The eyes of the fisherman are floating in the booze, and the booze is floating in the smoke. The cathedral clock strikes outside, the chimes last shorter than a hummed song, but nobody counts them, not even Adina.

Who did you tell the joke to, asks Paul.

That night, says Abi, I dreamed I was searching for my father's grave in a foreign city. I was led into a stone courtyard. The rear wall was the one my father was leaning against in that last picture. I had to cut a white ribbon. A tall fat man gave me a pair of scissors, and a small fat man in a white smock came next to me and stood on his tiptoes. He whispered into my ear that the courtyard was being consecrated. Then a line of men passed by one at a time. They were all very scrawny and had sightless eyes like glass balls. The small fat man asked, do you see him. I said, that can't be him. The small fat man said, you can't be sure, they're all already dead.

Paul and Abi are silent, resting their heads in their hands, the shattered minds inside their skulls. Tira-tira, tira-ta, the fisherman sings, and his mouth is in everyone's face. The bottle passes from hand to hand around the table. Each fisherman closes his eyes and drinks.

Inside the café, the evening takes its own time the same way this or that person takes his own life, just in passing, as a shadow in the river. It is winter in the city, a winter grown old and slow, a winter that pricks people with its cold. A winter in which mouths freeze and hands absently drop what they pick up, because fingertips thicken into leather. A city winter in which the water refuses to turn into ice, in which old people wear their past lives like coats. A winter in which young people hate one another like poison whenever they detect the slightest hint of happiness. And who nonetheless keep their eyes peeled while they go on searching for their lives. A winter walking along the river, where laughter freezes instead of the water. Where stuttering passes for speech and half-uttered words for loud shouts. Where every question dies away in the throat while silent tongues keep beating against clenched teeth.

The fisherman afraid of melons kisses the mouth of the bottle again and sings:

Once I used to sleep like a rock
Well all of me except my cock
Now it seems the reverse is true
My cock sleeps more than I ever do
Tira-tira tira-ta

The birthmark

The darkness is locked inside the stairwell and reeks of boiled cabbage. Even though the door to the building is open Adina cannot find the elevator. For the first few stairs the darkness clings to her legs, weighing them down. The flashlight's pale circle catches on the banister, then leaps soundlessly through the rails onto the wall. Her shoes clatter inside her head. On the second floor is a drying room, a handful of light from outside falls on a line of white diapers. The garbage chute next to the drying room is gray, like an arm made of cloth. On the third floor is a bare geranium in a plastic pot smelling of moldy earth and boiled cabbage. On the fourth floor she hears shoes squeaking. A pair of pant legs comes down the stairs, and a shirt bright enough to provide a little gleam. Adina raises her flashlight. The pale circle jumps onto the man's shoulder, half of his face, one eye, one ear, the white tips of his collar. And in the light, between his collar and his ear, is a birthmark. The edge of his nose. Then his chin which snaps the circle of light in two.

The market hall, Adina thinks, two nuts, his hand squeezing one against the other, and his voice asking what's your name. By this point he's reached the third floor, he's leaving and at the same time staying behind inside Adina's head. Back then it was summer, what are we going to do now, he asked. He's also the one who told the joke about the little Romanian. Abi said that his birthmark twitched on his jugular vein.

On the fifth floor the doorbell rings, Adina lifts her finger off the button, the bell goes silent, I know what I know, those were Clara's words, the door creaks, and Clara's rumpled hair is in the doorway.

Adina pushes in the door toward Clara's cheek, and Clara's hair moves back. Adina steps right past it, as though it were part of the doorway, and heads straight through the entrance hall. The door to the kitchen is open, the room smells of coffee.

Two cups on the tray, two spoons, grains of sugar scattered on the nightstand. The bed is unmade, the pattern in the damask pillowcase is like a breathy whisper.

He was here, says Adina, the man in the stairwell just now, that was Pavel. Clara's rumpled hair is dangling around her eyes, she pulls it back, her ears glow red beneath her thin fingers. You rarely see each other and rarely means every day, Adina's breath dogs every word, I know why you've been hiding him, she says, don't lie to me, your lawyer works for the Securitate. A hand towel is draped over the chair, right below Clara's arm, her thin fingers fasten the white round buttons on her blouse. Even if you don't say anything you're lying, says Adina. Red carnations are soaking in the vase, their stems touching, the water murky around the leaves.

I could never do anything to hurt you, says Clara, and neither could he. A pair of panty hose lies on the sewing machine. Adina clutches her chin and walks into the kitchen.

Clara leans against the refrigerator, puts a finger to her mouth. Pavel is a good person, she says, with closed lips. The coffeepot is askew on the burner, the stove top flecked with drops of coffee. He gave me his word, says Clara, he knows the only way I can love him is if nothing happens to you. A dish towel lies crumpled under the table. And my fox, says Adina, did he tell you why they're cutting up my fox. You realize that your good man is just carrying out orders, he's fucking you on assignment, in fact he wanted both of us, she says, one in the summer and one in the winter, he wakes up every morning and has two wishes in his head just like he has two eyes—for men it's his fist that gets hard and for women it's his cock.

Outside the apartment window a velvet skirt is hanging on the line, it's red and dry on top, black and wet on the bottom from the water dripping incessantly from the hem. And I'm sure that your good person promised all the others that he'd protect them too. Clara bites her lip, stares out the window straight past Adina. You don't know him, she says, pressing her hair against her head.

And you go to bed with a man like that, says Adina. The lid is off the sugar bowl, the sugar rock hard where the coffee spilled on it. The wind blows through the tree outside. You don't even know him, says Clara, the dented green ball is still stuck in the fork of the branches. I don't know you, says Adina. The dented green ball is submitting to another winter. The person I know isn't you, she says, I thought I knew you. Clara has scrunched up her toes, the cold rises off the floor tiles, coloring her knee blue, and passes into her stomach. You're sleeping with a criminal, Adina shouts, you're just like him, you're wearing him on your face, do you hear me, you're exactly the same. Clara warms one cold foot with the other. I don't ever want to see you again, Adina shouts, not ever. Her hands flail about, her eyes are gaping open, her gaze is a hunter that pounces out of her eyes and hits his mark. Her wet mouth screams and spews embers from her tongue. Her anger is hate, as black as her coat.

Stay here, says Clara. Adina brushes aside the thin fingers clutching at her coat and jerks away her sleeve. Don't touch me, she shouts, I can't bear the sight of your hands. Clara's hair stays in the kitchen, the hallway doesn't let her toes take a single step. The door slams shut.

The stairs race up along the wall, the flashlight tosses away its light. Adina's hand glides down the railing, clinging to it for support, the fourth floor, the third floor. The garbage chute rumbles, she hears something falling inside the shaft, something falling inside her head. Then the shattering of glass two floors below.

From underneath, the dented green ball in the fork of the tree is so small and dark it seems there's nothing up there, nothing except once again the eye. Coats pass by, inside them are not people but November. It's only the second week and already the month is so old and melancholy that evening arrives together with the morning.

My mother was always already my grandmother, Clara once said, not because of her age but because of how she handled it. She started to grow old, said Clara, when I was still a child. She hugged me tight and whispered in my ear, where are you my child, why are you so far away. And as she was growing old, her husband was staying young, said Clara, he got younger and younger compared to her. As if he were secretly watching her wilt away and preserving himself at her expense. And as if she, too, were allowing herself to wither for his sake. I don't want to be that way, said Clara, no one should be that way. And then his life sped up. What worked with her became his weakness. And then summer came to the city as though it were his first. He couldn't survive that first summer without her and died right after she did.

The stadium gate is open. Police and dogs are waiting in the parking lot. Men come surging out of the gate singing and shouting. Inside the stadium the Danes couldn't stop the Romanian ball and the Romanian ball won. Light rises from the stadium's earthen wall as though the moon had lost its way. Who the hell are the Danes now, the men shout as they carry their tricolor flags with their three distinct stripes. The hungry red, the mute yellow, and the spied-on blue stripes in the cut-off land. Who the hell's heard of the Danes now, the men's lips speak words like world and World Cup, their singing creeps up their throats, like the brambles on the earthen wall of the stadium. What the hell do the Danes want here. The long-distance runner looks on indifferently. When crowds go wild he stands all alone, a stranger.

Awaken, Romanian, wake from thy deadly slumber, sings an elderly man. The old anthem is forbidden, the man stands on the curb and sees the muzzle of a dog and the shoes of a policeman. He lifts his chin high and sings to distance himself from his fear. He tears his fur cap off his head, waves it, hurls it to the ground and tramples it with his shoes. And tramples and tramples and sings and sings so that the song can be heard in the soles of his shoes. And the song is forbidden and the song smells of brandy. The flags overhead are raving mad, the heads of the men below are drunk, the shoes confused. The flags accompany the men on the street as they walk into the night.

The old man's voice falters. My god, he says, standing by the bare acacia, what we could be in the world, and here we don't even have bread to eat. A policeman with a dog goes up to him, and another policeman. The man throws up his arms and shouts up to heaven, God forgive us for being Romanians. His eyes shine in the sparse light, a hasty shine in the corner of the eye. The dog yelps and pounces on his neck. Two, three, five policemen carry him away.

The parking lot rises and falls, and with it the bare acacia. The steps from the street bounce across his face. The parking lot is standing on its head. The sky is the Danube down below, the asphalt is the night above. In the upside-down gaze, white light spreads over the city, there below the earthen wall, up in the sky, in the cut-off land.

The head of the old man hangs all the way down.

The wasp game

By morning loneliness has already left its mark on the face of the child with eyes set far apart and narrow temples. He's sitting on a bench right in the middle of other children but he is alone. His eyes are red, the brown rings of his pupils faded.

Twice during class Adina is tempted to call the child to the blackboard. She can tell by the way he's staring out the window that his thoughts aren't stopping at the pane. His gaze is clearly one with much to think about. Instead she calls on the child sitting right in front of the absent boy. And then on the one sitting next to him. The boy's eyes are so far apart they don't notice.

After class the child sits on the window ledge and yawns. He tells Adina that last night his mother took him to some place in back of the cathedral, two streets past the bridge. That's where the Hungarian priest lives, he says, a lot of people were praying and singing. There were police and soldiers there too, but they weren't praying and singing, just watching. It was cold and dark, says the child. My mother told me that you don't ever feel cold when you pray and sing. That's why the people weren't cold. And also because of the candles. Their faces and hands were all lit up, my hands were lit up too, says the child. When you hold a candle in front of your chin the light shines through your throat and through your hand. The child raises his left hand and splays the fingers against the glass. The policemen and the soldiers were cold, says the child. Adina sees the gray wart clusters on his fingers. The poplars jag upward into the sky, sharp and bare. My mother said that even where nobody's around there can still be someone there, just like sometimes in summer you see a shadow where there isn't anything or anybody, says the child. My mother said that places like that are drawers you don't see and can't open. She said there are drawers like that in the tree trunks, in the grass, in the fence, in the walls. With a piece of greenish chalk in his right hand the boy traces his left hand on the window-pane. And each of these drawers has an ear inside, my mother said. He takes his hand off the window, leaving the outline of a see-through hand. These ears are always listening, my mother said. Whenever anybody comes to visit us my mother puts the phone in the refrigerator, says the boy. He laughs, the laughter flits away from his face. He rests his head on the hand holding the chalk. I never put the phone in the refrigerator, he says.

The boy draws green fingernails on the see-through fingers. Below the fingernails he chalks in a few green warts where the outline was wobbly.

The sky is gray, but gray is not a color, because everything is gray. The apartment blocks in the distance are also gray, but a different gray than the day, differently colorless.

You don't have any warts, Comrade Teacher, the boy says to

Adina, because when you grow up the warts go away, they pass on to the children. My mother once told me that when your warts go away then your troubles start to come.

Warm steam comes out of the child's mouth. It is invisible. Outside, under the jagged poplars, it would be visible. It would hover silently in the air for a moment before drifting away. What the mouth had just said would be seen in the air. But that wouldn't change anything. Because what would be seen in the air would be there just for itself and not available. The way everything in the streets is just for itself and not available, the way the city is just for itself, the people in the city just for themselves. The only thing that's there for everybody is this splitting cold.

The greenish berries stayed on the windowpane, clustered on the see-through fingers.

The wedding procession is small. First comes the tractor, then the musicians, then the rest. The civil registry office is in the House of Youth, just one block beyond the earthen wall of the stadium. Six policemen are walking alongside the procession. Weddings are forbidden, they claim, because assemblies are forbidden. So they simply invited themselves as guests.

The stadium gate is closed, the Danes are back in Denmark, but the forbidden song has spread and is now being sung throughout the city.

During the night the dogs were barking everywhere, all throughout the city streets, sounding closer than they usually do in a snowless winter, when the night is its own echo. And people were on the move as the night progressed, when the only thing keeping it in the city was the cold. And they stayed out later than the last way home. They cut across streets carrying their flashlights. And where they stopped the flashlights went out and match flames flared and died away on their fingers. And candles were lit.

Adina follows herself home. At the corner, by the thick spool of wire, a rusty streak is crawling across the road, it's the metal seeping away from the wire due to all the freezing and thawing, and with no snow to keep it hidden. The dog OLGA barks in front of the wooden shed, green berries light up in her eyes. OLGA, Adina says out loud. Inside the dog's head is a drawer that doesn't open. The day is locked up inside this skull, rolled back into this nightly barking. The path knows its own way and has no distance. Each of Adina's steps is alike and each is wobbly.

Then her shoes begin to hurry, her head is empty, even though the fox is lurking inside. The fox is always lurking inside her head.

Whenever Adina comes from the street into her apartment, her cold fingertips flush with heat as soon as she looks in the bathroom. Afterward her shoe shoves the tail and two hind legs away from the fur. Every day.

A cigarette is floating in the toilet bowl, not yet swollen from the water. Adina now shifts her foot to the fox's right foreleg. It moves together with the tip of her shoe, leaving the neck exactly where it was.

Her heart pounds and the pounding rises into her mouth as her fingers shove the cut appendages back against the belly.

Pavel could have been a groomsman, but ever since the game against the Danes the crowds haven't put away their flags and don't go home at night. So he had to decline since he's on duty day and night. Where the hell do they come from anyway, he said, they all have thin skin and don't get any sun. Judging from the way they look they must live up where the planet starts to shrink.

The clarinets rip through the wedding song, the violins can barely hold on to the thin melody between the apartment blocks, where the narrow space creates an echo. The accordion opens and closes in step. Clara pulls her thin heel out of a crack in the asphalt. The groom's carnation is broken, the stem sticks out of his buttonhole.

The tractor's bucket is in the air, the teeth in front covered with soil. The wedding couple is standing inside the giant shovel. The bride's veil flutters, her white carnations quiver at every pothole. Her white sleeves are dirty. The dwarf is wearing a black suit and a white shirt and a black bow tie. His new shoes have heels as high as two broken bricks. Grigore wears a large hat, the gatewoman a headscarf with a red silk fringe. The gateman is carrying a ring cake. His eyes are moist, he sings:

Your childhood now has passed away
From this day on it's always May

The bride is Mara. For two years she's been waiting for this day, and now assemblies are forbidden.

We're getting married, not doing anything political, the groom told the policemen.

The bite on Mara's leg has long since healed. For weeks she showed it off every morning in the office. First it was red, then it grew bigger and turned blue. When it turned green the bite was larger than ever. Then the teeth vanished into her skin. And the wound turned yellow, frayed away, shrank and disappeared.

Mara had troubles with her fiancé. He wanted to break off the engagement. She had to show him the spot every evening, and he got used to it. But he refused to believe the bite came from the director. He said, if I could only be sure those teeth weren't GRIGORE'S.

Snow geese need the snow that doesn't come. At least not here. They contort their necks and open their beaks. They scream. They flounder on the flat ground. After the night frost has melted they splay their wings. It's difficult, but they take a running start and lift off when they spread out their webbing. The air flaps and ripples close to the grass, then the air over the trees, like leaves whooshing in the bare forest. Once in flight across the sky, the snow geese spread out in formation and let the plain, the field and the corn fall away from their wings, smaller and smaller. There is no snow, but once they've been to a place, the terrain is mapped inside them forever, a white sphere. And down below the blackish green hill rises out of the ground. Feathers fly in their wake for a long time after they have passed.

The crows stay in the forest because the forest is black. The branches pretend to be dead.

The soldiers play the wasp game. They stand in a circle. Whoever is the crane fly has to stand in the middle and cover his eyes tight with his hands so he can't see. There can't be any gap. All the others are the wasps. They all hum in a circle around the crane fly and one of them stings him with a blow to the hand. The crane fly has to guess which wasp stung him. If he takes too long to guess he gets stung again, and again. The crane fly tries to guess, the crane fly is afraid. He keeps his hands pressed to his head, each hit hurts more and more. Every time he gets stung the crane fly falls to the ground. Then he has to get up and look at all the wasps and guess which one stung him, over and over until he can't get up anymore. And even longer. And meanwhile the wasps' lips quiver and hum.

When the crane fly can no longer stand, he is allowed to be a wasp.

Every crane fly stays lying in the dirt well after the last sting, without moving. The officer with the gold tooth nudges him with the tip of his boot. When the crane fly finally stands up to join the wasps, his eyes are ringed with bruises, and every bone aches.

Today Ilie is lucky, he doesn't have to be the crane fly.

Every Sunday afternoon during the summer I give my son a ten-lei coin, the officer says. His eyes are glued to the sky, he's following the snow geese, there's snow in the mountains, he says, they're changing their course.

He swallows. My son, he says, doesn't let the coin out of his hand even when he's putting on his white sandals. Then we take our car into town. I go to the summer garden and drink beer and my son takes my ID and goes around the corner to the Party Cafeteria, he really likes cake. The officer smacks his gold tooth. The cakes are in the display case, which is so tall that last summer it was still only at eye height for him. Since then he's grown a lot, says the officer, next summer he'll be able to see the cakes better. His favorite is the one with the bright green icing, he says. But he's scared of the bees in the cafeteria so he closes his eyes. And the cook says to him every time, bees make the cake sweet.

The officer exhales, his breath gray in the air. They're really wasps, not bees, he says, and they like the raspberry icing best. Every summer the cook's hand is swollen blue from all the stings, it's creepy. When he serves he has to drape a white towel over his hand. That's the odd thing, says the officer, the bees always buzzing around the beer in the summer garden don't sting. His gold tooth shines. But with the cakes in the Party Cafeteria it's the wasps, he says.

Ilie looks up at the blackish-green hill and senses for just a moment that the officer's face is very pale, and that the gold tooth is a yellow beak. The beak of a snow goose.

When the tank has been sitting in the forest for weeks, when the trenches have been finished for days, when the officer with the gold tooth is weary from spending half the season in the barrack and sick of looking at the sandbags in the yard, the column marches out along the path up to the field and through the broken corn and over the hill to play the wasp game.

The snow geese flounder on the ground. They bring the cold with them, who knows where from, they screech and pull in their wings. They always fly far away. There they eat snow. They always come back, but they never eat grass or corn. When they aren't flying they keep away from the forest and stand there and look up at the sky.

The wasp game is a good equalizer, a beautiful contest, says the officer. He doesn't play with the men, he only watches. The rules of the game shine on his gold tooth. Turn around, he says to the crane fly. And now hum, he says to the wasps. He has them hum for as long as he wants. Sting, sting, he shouts, and sting hard like a wasp, not like a flea.

The spreading city

The woman with the chestnut-red hair done up in big waves is cleaning her windows. Beside her is a bucket of steaming water. She reaches into the bucket and picks up a sopping gray rag, she reaches onto the windowsill and picks up a moist gray rag, then she pulls a dry white cloth off her shoulder. After that she bends over and picks up some crumpled pieces of newsprint. The windowpanes shine, her hair opens up into two sections, divided by the open casements. When she closes the casements she closes her hair.

The frost has darkened the petunias, knotting their leaves and stems in a tangle of black. When the weather warms the frozen petunias will stick to one another.

The woman waits until the sun above the stadium sends out warm rays for two weeks in a row, then she goes to the market to buy new petunias. They are packed in newspaper and perched on the windowsill. The woman digs out the old black plants, using a large knife to pry the deep roots out of the window box. Then she takes a very large nail and aerates the soil, and unwraps the new petunias one by one. Their roots are short and hairy. She widens the holes in the dirt with the nail and sticks the hair inside the holes. She closes the holes with her fingers. Then she waters the new white petunias so much that the flower box drips for two days.

The first night helps rearrange the stems and leaves of the freshly planted petunias, so they no longer can be seen in the morning when the big-waved hair appears in the window. The daylight brings warmth, the petunias bloom for themselves. Every day the marks of winter crawl farther and farther below the white flowers and underneath the city.

The poplars and acacias let their bare bark shimmer green before they sprout leaves. Then the cold is gone and everything is exposed. That's when the dictator climbs into the helicopter and flies over the country. Over the plains, over the Carpathians. His old man's legs are riding high in the sky, up where the wind emerges to dry the winter out of the fields.

Wherever a glacial lake flashes in the sun, the servant's daughter said to Adina, and the reflection shines back up into his eyes, he reaches out his hand. He shifts his old legs and says, corn doesn't grow in water, that lake has to be dried out.

He has a house in every city, and every city shrinks between his temples as his helicopter touches down. Wherever he lands, he spends the night. Wherever he spends the night, a bus with boarded-up windows passes slowly through the streets. The bus is full of wire cages. It stops in front of every building to collect all the roosters and dogs and haul them away. Nothing is allowed to awaken the dictator except for light, said the servant's daughter, any crowing or barking throws him off. For instance, she said, say he's scheduled to give a speech from the balcony of the opera. And suddenly his old legs stop in the middle of town and he has to close his eyes for a moment simply because some rooster jarred his sleep by crowing, or because some dog barked. Then when he opens his eyes and the black inside sees the opera standing there, he might stretch out his hand and say, housing blocks don't grow in an opera, that opera has to be torn down.

He hates opera, said the servant's daughter. The officer's wife heard from the wife of an officer in the capital that the dictator once went to the opera. And that he said, this is nothing but a stage full of people and instruments, you can hardly hear a thing. One guy plays while the others all just sit there, he said. Then he stretched out his hand. And the next day the orchestra was dissolved.

According to the wife from the capital the dictator puts on new underclothes every morning, said the servant's daughter. Also a new suit, a new shirt, a new tie, new socks, new shoes, all sealed in transparent bags, so that no one can put poison on them. And every morning in the winter he has a new coat, a new scarf, a new fur cap or a new hat. As if the clothes from the day before had become too small because his power grew in the night while he slept.

In life his face is shrinking but on the pictures it gets bigger and bigger, his forelock is graying but in the pictures it's blacker and blacker.

The dictator's discarded clothes wander through the land like darkness while the old man's legs are sleeping. And black caps worn during the day bring out the moon at night, according to the servant's daughter.

And these moons are always white, never yellow. Or at most they are half-white, with a mouth gaping and yawning into the sky. A moon that makes dogs howl and drives their glowing eyes deep into their head when the cathedral bell prepares to strike twelve. A moon with a cheek looming a little too close on the way home. A highwayman of the night, a gap in the darkness behind the last streetcar.

Where a person climbs out at night and never comes home, there are empty paving stones in the morning.

Outside the window a last bit of light sneaks along its hidden path. The floor is dark, the fox is brighter, stretching out its cut-off paws. A person could fling open the window and if the wind blew inside, the wall would start to flutter, it could be pushed in with a finger just like a curtain, just like standing water. Ilie knows this, he thinks every day about his watery plain, his soft way out. He has chewed his grass straw and swallowed it. He has taken his mouth out of the picture, placed a mark on his cheek like liver mortis, a mark Adina cannot touch with her finger.

Adina lifts her hands off the table. Where they were resting the table is warm. And down on the floor, where the fox is the hunter, her fingers slide the cut-off legs against the fur. And after her hands have once again warmed the table, they clasp her forehead. Her hands sense that her forehead is as warm as the table, but unlike the table it no longer knows anything about inhabiting a place, abiding.

The bell rings in several long bursts, startling the apartment. Adina peers through the peephole. Clara is standing outside the door, I can see your eye, she says, open up. Adina moves away, the door's eye is empty, then covered by Clara's eye. Clara's fist bangs on the door, I know you're there, she says. Adina leans against the wall. In the hallway the buckles on Clara's purse clink against the floor. Paper crinkles.

A note passes through the crack of the door.

Adina reads:

PEOPLE ARE BEING ARRESTED THERE ARE LISTS YOU HAVE TO HIDE NO ONE WILL LOOK FOR YOU AT MY PLACE

The neighbor's door opens and closes. Clara's high heels clatter on the stairs. Adina drags the note away from the door with the tip of her shoe. She bends over, reads it one more time. She crumples the note, throws it into the toilet. It floats, the water swamps the paper but doesn't swallow it. Then Adina's hand reaches into the water, takes the note, smooths it out, folds it, sticks it in her coat pocket.

The wardrobe is open. The suitcase on the carpet is open. A nightgown goes flying past the suitcase and lands on the fox. A sweater and a pair of pants land in the suitcase. A towel, a knot of panty hose and panties, a toothbrush, a nail clipper, a comb.

The hospital blocks the end of the street, presenting a row of small lit windows, a chain of moons that merge into the sky without transition, without a single star. A car pulls up with two men inside and a tiny child's shoe swinging from the rearview mirror. The headlights angle their beams onto the ground. Adina turns her face away. When the motor stops, her heart can surely be heard pounding through her coat. The beams cut the suitcase from her hand. The men go in the hospital.

The entrance to the hospital has a tall flight of stairs with bushes planted on both sides. Adina stashes her suitcase in the bushes. The bushes are bare. While she's reaching into the shrubbery her hand jerks twice, but it's just a forgotten leaf, moist and withered. The suitcase is far below the stairs, the wind is dark, heavier than the leaves. She climbs the steps.

Adina waits with her hands hidden in her coat. She doesn't give the gateman her name, he'll see me when he gets here, she says. The gateman telephones. Her right hand feels the wet note in her coat pocket.

The gateman paces up and down. He peers through the glass booth—a few stairs, a bit of night and a faded sound settle in his eyes, which having felt the power of the binoculars can withstand anything. His shoes creak. Two wrinkles run from his cheeks all the way inside his mouth. The ceiling lamp does not shed light, it only watches. The bushes are brighter in the gateman's eyes than they are outside, because the centers of his eyes are glowing, and each has a lightbulb right in the middle.

Paul comes down the stairs, his white cap is a large petunia that swallows his left ear. Adina places the wet note in his hand. The paper is crumpled, with more ridges and wrinkles than his outstretched thumb.

As Paul reads, the gateman studies the night as is his habit, all ears and furtive eyes. Outside, wind rattles the metal sign. Wait inside the car, says Paul, standing on the granite floor in his white cloth shoes. He places two keys in her palm, they are wrapped in white sterile gauze. So they don't clink, he says, when you get outside count the windows, my car's parked just past the tenth one. Take off your white shoes, says Adina, they're too visible. He looks at the floor, I know that once I'm outside I'm no longer a doctor, he says. His white coat is made of chalk, freshly starched and ironed.

Her hands are no longer afraid of the shrub, even if the leaves inside are wet and withered. Adina is carrying her suitcase in front of her, with both hands, so that it disappears inside her coat. On the path that can't be seen in the dark she counts the windows above the shrubbery, from one to the next she can make out the individual branches in the wind.

The car door clicks. Adina puts her suitcase on the backseat. She wonders where the little nail clipper has crawled to among all the thick clothing. Next to the suitcase is Anna's scarf. A car pulls up to the entrance. Two policemen come out the front doors, two dogs out the back. They smell the asphalt, sniff at the steps. Sitting in the car, Adina would like to shrink, to be as tiny as the nail clipper in her suitcase.

Paul comes out of the bright doorway and goes down the stairs, his shoes are dark. Like a night watchman he paces past the bushes, looking up at the windows. His pants blend in with the pavement.

He knocks on the window, the door opens, his legs are his only luggage. What are the police looking for, and the dogs, Adina asks. He turns the key, the car hums. Every night they bring the wounded from the border, he says, most are dead. First we're driving to Abi's then out to Liviu's in the country.

The street runs by, the city is a black thimble with steep sides, the housing blocks as narrow as foreheads. There's a workshop next to the morgue, says Paul, where the coffins are sealed and sent home under police watch. No one ever bothers to look inside, says Paul.

The window a few stories up is lit. Paul doesn't ring, he only knocks once on the door, Abi opens, laughs and raises his eyebrows, he smells of brandy. Adina hands him the note, Paul grabs him by the arm, come on, he says, we're driving out to the country. Abi's eyes are blank, too large and too small for his face, he nods. Then he breaks away, no, I'm not going, he says, and I don't want to know what place you're thinking of. Good luck, he says. What's that supposed to mean. Good luck, the village is a small place.

At the black street corners people are walking, carrying flashlights. The night takes away their clothes, Paul drives slowly, Paul drives quietly.

For a while Adina imagines that because the forbidden song has spread, the city has no limits. That the streets extend farther and farther out into the country and wherever they go they take the city with them. That somewhere out in the dark fields, when the road turns, the bells will ring because the forest beyond the frozen corn is really a city park, beyond which is the cathedral tower, and that the river is creeping right down the middle of what only seems to be an empty field.

And she imagines that the dictator has seen the spreading city from high in the air, and that he's ordered the army to surround it. And that the soldiers are shoveling away, cutting off the spreading city, building a moat without a single bridge. That Ilie too is digging and digging and signaling to her, raising and lowering his fingers like waves, stepping on his spade with his boots, pushing it into the city's edge and thinking about the Danube.

And she imagines Paul climbing into the car wearing his white shoes, and driving and driving until the city stops and the last light at the edge of town is extinguished, and then not saying another word. And that while down below a field is blundering about with no sense of boundaries, Paul is intent on gazing at the sky, in search of a white moon.

The chamber pot

Paul's hand passes across Adina's face.

She startles. We're here, says Paul. Adina feels a trickle of sand inside her head. She pulls Paul's heavy hand off her cheek, was I asleep, she asks as she opens her eyes, her face is awry, her cheeks caved in.

The bench outside Liviu's house is lower on one end. There is a puddle where the legs are sinking into the mud. The window looms dark behind the fence. The gate is locked.

In the south, in the part of the country cut off by the Danube, the houses are lined up along the road, road and village are one and the same. Here the settlement doesn't spread, each fence is connected to the next, each house has a garden in back, and each garden ends with a clearly defined border. There's no place for dogs to roam, no place for them to bark. The villagers keep lots of dogs, Liviu told Paul and Adina during the summer, but not on account of robbers, theft is not a problem. It's so they won't hear the gunshots. And they keep geese instead of roosters, he said, because geese gaggle throughout the night.

But it doesn't work because the villagers have gotten so used to the barking and gaggling that they no longer hear it, while they do hear the gunshots.

Adina listens, the geese gaggle short and low in the yard, and in the yard next door, and in the yard across the road. The geese are kept in pens covered with boards. They can be heard stamping their feet and beating their wings against the wood. They're so cramped they knock into one another and are never able to truly fall asleep. A roadside village is long and narrow like a sock, like the neck of a goose.

During the summer Liviu became a bridegroom. He married a teacher from the village because he was an outsider and all on his own. His wife is young, not even close to his age. Liviu listens in silence, just for himself, because his wife is used to women doing the talking while the men sit nearby, just for themselves. She grew up with the gunshots, with the dogs and with the geese.

During the summer, when Adina and Paul went to Liviu's wedding, this young woman in her white veil and long dress had the face of a lamb. A lamb that had yet to eat grass, Paul said at the time. Everyone hugged and kissed her while Liviu just shook their hands and looked away. At the wedding she ate a lot, while Liviu chewed his food absentmindedly. Liviu danced as if he had stones in his pockets, while she danced as if her white dress were a flying feather. She didn't speak much, and whenever she did she smiled. The village policeman got so drunk he was laughing all alone at his own jokes, repeating the same sentence that no one understood. And the village priest set his cap on the neck of a bottle, there were soup noodles stuck in his gray beard. After the meal he lifted his cassock up to his knee and danced with the policeman. Liviu looked at Adina and Paul, when are you two getting married, he asked. Paul said, soon. Adina could feel the lie running across her face. She pointed at the policeman and asked the lamb, are you related. Liviu didn't say anything, the young lamb smiled and said, that's the way it is here in the country, the policeman's included along with everyone else.

Paul picks up a few pebbles. He tosses them at the window, they scratch against the glass and then rustle when they land on the dry leaves. They're sound asleep, says Paul. The dogs bark louder, the geese are mute. Paul scales the fence and raps on the window with his fingers. A light snaps on in the last window.

Liviu's head is squashed from sleep. The casement creaks open, it's me, says Paul. He raises his chin, his face can't be seen in the dark, we have to hide, he says. Liviu recognizes Paul's voice.

They roll the car into the barn. Liviu covers it with straw and uses sacks to hide the wheels. White wings and feathers shine through the cracks of the pen, the geese inside gaggle, their beaks bang against the wood.

The lamb comes to the stairs wearing her nightgown and shoes that are too large for her bare feet. She points her flashlight at the barn, but the circle of light gets stopped by its own reflection in a puddle.

Inside the kitchen, in the light, the lamb smiles. We were just talking about you yesterday, says Liviu. We were just talking about you, says the lamb, and here you show up on our doorstep. Adina sets her bag down next to the oven, Paul reaches in his jacket and sets a toothbrush on the table, that's all the luggage I have, he says.

The lamb shows Adina into a dark room and closes the flowered curtains, patterned with the same dense bouquets of roses as on the tablecloth. Here's the flashlight, she says, don't turn the big light on, that can be seen from outside. She squeezes some clothes together inside the wardrobe, everyone knows which room we sleep in, I've made some space for your clothes, she says.

It's the same room, the same bed as in the summer. As they lay in bed early in the morning after the wedding Adina asked Paul, why did you lie. Paul sighed, mosquitoes flitted around the light. Why does Liviu think we're still together. Paul yawned and said, is that so important.

It had rained the previous morning, the day of the wedding. After that it was scorching hot, the night didn't cool things off, they had to keep the window open. Adina turned off the light, the crickets chirped their jittery notes throughout the village. Paul fell asleep before he could close his mouth. As he slept he took the covers off his legs and snored all the way into his toes. He and Liviu had had plenty to drink, and had gotten into a long discussion with a toothless accountant about the falling protein content in the milk from the national cows. The mosquitos didn't like the smell of brandy and only attacked Adina's face. The folk music was still turning inside her head.

During that mosquito night Adina dreamed that she was dancing in the yard with the toothless accountant. A spoon was lying on the ground, and the accountant kept stepping on it. She pulled him away, closer to the edge of the garden. But there was another spoon near the edge of the garden, and he kept stepping on that one as well. And a withered lady who was even older than the accountant sat with her back to the table and watched them. Now dance decently, she told the accountant, the lady comes from the city.

The flashlight rummages through the dark bag, the comb is on top, the nail clipper on the bottom, the toothbrush between the stockings. The nightgown feels cold to the touch. Their armpits smell of sweat, and so do their feet. Paul holds his toothbrush handle in his mouth. Liviu places a white chamber pot next to the bed, don't go out in the yard, he says, not during the day either.

Paul lets the toothbrush drop from his mouth onto the table, he walks around the table, shines the flashlight on one of the tablecloth bouquets. Dogs bark outside, Paul sniffs the roses on the curtain, may I set my shoes next to yours, he asks, then shines the light on Adina's shoes and sets his beside hers. He lies down on the bed fully dressed and laughs.

I have to go, says Adina, she takes the chamber pot, there's no face inside the bed, only Paul's clothes. I wanted to go earlier, while we were in the barn, she says. I went three times on the way here, I was so scared, says Paul. She shines the light in the chamber pot, it's brand-new, the worst thing is the sound, she says. Well I am a musician, says Paul. She shoves the chamber pot between her legs, I'll whistle, he says, my grandfather didn't get along with his brother-in-law, he would stop his horses in front of the man's house and whistle until they pissed, then he'd drive on. Paul hears a rushing sound, and Adina feels a warm mist against her calves. A newspaper is lying on the table. Adina covers the chamber pot with it and listens. Hanging behind the curtain is wind, it shakes the bare branches. I imagined the sound differently, says Paul.

We had a summer latrine and a winter one and four chamber pots, says Adina. The summer latrine was behind our grapevines in a dry little patch, the winter one was tucked away by the entrance to the cellar. The summer latrine was made of boards, the winter one was made of stone. My chamber pot was red, my mother's green and my father's was blue. The fourth was made of glass, it was the prettiest but it was never used. That's only for guests, my mother said. We never had guests, only visitors who stopped in for just a while. The seamstress came two or three times a year to bring my mother a dress, she would eat two rolls without sitting down and after that she would leave. And now and then in the fall, when my father managed to get plum brandy from the village where they had the sheep, the barber would come over. He would drink three glasses without sitting down and after that he would leave. My father suggested a couple times that the barber could give him a quick haircut. The barber said, I can only do that in the shop. I need a mirror, when I cut hair I have to be able to see myself as well as you.

All the people who visited us lived in the same dirty outskirts of town. No one was a guest, no one stayed overnight, says Adina. Paul says nothing. He's fallen asleep in his clothes, without a face.

The fingernails grow

I remembered it and then I forgot it, says a woman's voice next to the window. The rose bouquets in the curtains are larger during the day. The geese outside also sound different than at night, their honking is brighter. Adina watches them form a long white line from one end of the village to the other, all the way into the field, where the frozen corn swallows them one by one and doesn't let them get away, as long as their feathers are warm. And Adina thinks: from one end of the village to the other, the people are lined up at their windows watching the corn swallow the geese. They aren't startled, because they're used to the gunshots. They're simply astonished to see the frozen cornstalks straying into the village, from one end to the other.

Paul's face is lying on the pillow, gray, older than in the city. His clothes are crumpled from the day before. On top of the wardrobe is a row of canning jars full of whole apricots that look like stones. The jars are covered with cellophane tied off with green thread. Adina feels a chill inside her skull, she taps her forehead. Her toothbrush is next to Paul's, and next to that is the nail clipper. She picks up her toothbrush and holds the handle in her mouth.

In front of the wardrobe Adina's toes can feel the fox even though there's nothing but the rug's white fringe. She closes her eyes and slips her bare feet into her shoes. She sniffs her handkerchief. Then she takes the chamber pot into the kitchen.

Embers are glowing in the stove. On the kitchen table is bacon and a loaf of bread, and next to that a note: WE'LL BE BACK AT 12.

Inside Adina's head the days form a line without a village, endlessly long, made of bed and curtains and chamber pot and kitchen. Concealed like a spine running from the back of her neck to the tips of her fingers. The days are both short and long. Her ears are more awake than her eyes, which know everything the house contains. Being constantly on the alert for every sound can cause fear to be read as absentmindedness.

No radio and no TV unless we're home, Liviu said, the neighbors can hear.

If a voice calls out near the gate, and the man pulling up the latch is wearing a uniform in the crack between the curtains, Adina and Paul move to the door farthest in the back. They stand jammed together in the pantry until they no longer hear anything. Afterward a newspaper is lying on the front steps, or the mail has been delivered. When Liviu and the lamb come back from school, they lay the newspaper on the kitchen table. And on the first page is the forelock and the black inside the eye. And underneath, the news that the most beloved son of the people has fled to Iran, and days later the news that he has returned from Iran and is back in the country.

And Adina thinks that her ears ought to smooth themselves out from all the listening, lose their lobes and curlicues to become as smooth and flat as the palms of her hands, that they ought to grow fingers that could twitch as fast as fear. Only the rushing in the chamber pot offers some variety, the sound is different every time, Paul always takes longer than she does, he plays with his stream and is able to fake a laugh about the yellow foam. Only when he has to shit does he curse and agonize over his constipation and say that he feels like a louse hiding in the edge of a bed.

The newspaper on the chamber pot is always yesterday's, and Paul always places it with the forelock facing down. And shortly afterward he shoves a few logs and dry corncobs into the stove and stares at the fire far too long, while peeking out the corner of his eye from under his arm. Because Adina is lathering herself with soap and her breasts are dangling naked over the washbowl. And she knows that Paul will take hold of them with his cold hands and glowing hot face. She is waiting for it and she can't stand it. And then their faces appear in the linden blossom tea, his aged and hers empty, separated by the spoon handles, each in its own cup. And both spoons stir until the sugar melts. I still haven't heard any shots, Paul says, I hear the dogs bark and the geese cackle and the mailman calling at the gate but no shots. I keep listening for something loud, though I understand from Liviu that the shots are quiet, like a branch breaking, only different.

At one point a key turned in the door, and Liviu hauled a long sack into the kitchen containing a Christmas tree that couldn't be obtained in the roadside village, a slender silver fir that a student's father who drives a truck stole along a forest road in the Carpathians. That was yesterday, says Paul, and Adina says, no, that was this morning. Liviu left the sack by the wall and had to go right back out, to attend a meeting, he said. He locked the door from the outside, and Paul pulled the sack off the fir tree, the needles looked brittle and gray in the kitchen. Put it back in the sack, said Adina, I can't bear looking at it.

Yesterday was something else. The nail clipper snipped and Adina saw the curved tip of her nail drop onto the table. Ever since they've been cutting the fox, my nails grow faster, she said. Paul gave his fake laugh, she stuck her forefinger in her mouth and pulled the rest of the nail off with her teeth, then bit it into tiny pieces and ate it. I see it every day at school, how hair and nails grow faster with the neglected children than with the ones who are looked after, she said. When you live in fear, your hair and nails grow faster, you can tell by looking at the children, the shaven backs of their necks. Paul cut some bacon into transparent slices and rolled them on his lips before swallowing. As a doctor I have to contradict you, he said, pointing at the forelock in the newspaper. If that were the case, his hair would grow all the way from the forehead down to the toes in a single day. He polished his fingernails with thin slices of bacon until they glistened. What do you know about people, said Adina, the ones you work on are either sick or dead, what do you see when you cut them open. Nothing. Is there a medical explanation for a dictator, is the dictatorness found in the brain, the stomach, the liver or in the lungs. Paul stopped his ears with his shiny fingernails and raised his voice, it's found deep in the heart, just like inside your novels.

The forelock keeps growing, thought Adina, day by day, all the way down to his toes, the sack containing his hair has long been full, stamped down and stuffed to the top and heavier than the man himself. He deceives everyone, even the barber.

And the day before yesterday the soup was in the bowl, and Paul wanted to call Adina to eat, and called out ABI instead of Adina. Then while the two were silent the soup sat in the bowl and grew a thin skin that stuck to the spoon. And Paul said, you know who Abi told that joke about the little Romanian to. Who, she asked, and Paul said: Ilie.

Adina stared at her bowl, the blobs of fat stayed round, not even the spoon could break them up. For the first time Adina heard a noise. It was not a dog and not a goose, like a branch breaking, only entirely different. It was inside her own head.

And on that same day in the evening, or maybe the evening after, the lamb brought a little bag of chocolates for the Christmas tree. Each piece was wrapped in red tinfoil and had a silk thread for hanging. From a nurse, said the lamb, her son is in my class. She took one piece and popped the whole thing into her mouth and let it melt silently on her tongue. There are times when Liviu wants to move back to the city, she said, but now it's good that we're out here, at the end of the world, as Liviu calls it. Here everybody knows what his neighbor had for dinner two days ago, said the lamb, what he buys and sells and how much money he has. And how much brandy is in his cellar, said Liviu. She ate another piece of chocolate, then she started carving up a goose, cutting the drumsticks from the body, the wings from the breast cavity. I simply try not to stick out, said Liviu, and it's the same at school. I just listen and think what I think. The lamb lifted the goose by the long neck and slit open the stomach. It was full of little stones. I know that's selfish, that I'm only looking after myself, said Liviu, but otherwise you wouldn't be here now. How long can you stay in hiding, asked the lamb, placing some bay leaves on the table.

Is there some other place in this country where you could live, asked Liviu. Adina peeled potatoes and Paul watched the peel coil off between her thumb and the knife.

Are you suggesting we set off across the field and head toward the Danube, asked Adina, should we try to escape, do you want to hear shots and guess it's probably us. In less than half an hour we'd be lying out there in the wheat until the harvester comes. Paul tugged Adina by the shoulders and she said right in his face, and then the accountant will have an explanation for the rising protein content of the flour. Paul stopped her mouth. She pushed his hand away and saw the potatoes start to blur. And every now and then, she said, a hair will get stuck in your teeth while you're eating, and it won't be one of the baker's that just happened to land in the dough.

Transparent sleep

After the evening with the cut-up goose, everyone went to bed without a word and all but Adina slept very deeply, because they took the hair found in the bread into their sleep. Sleep crept so deeply inside them during the night because it was ashamed of the evening.

Before she went to bed Adina laid her nightgown on the table and said, I'm not getting undressed, I'm cold. She took her coat out of the wardrobe and laid it over the blanket. Paul dozed off, distanced from himself and dejected. The idea of sleep didn't occur to Adina, though, she was so alert her eyes filled the entire room. She lay there waiting without moving while Paul breathed calmly in his sleep.

Then she slipped into her shoes and pulled on her coat. She wanted to get away, walk down the road, not to the border, only as far as the cornfield. Maybe I could lie down there, she thought, and freeze to death. Ilie had told her that the cold comes up through the toes and that by the time it reaches your stomach it no longer hurts. After that everything happens quickly. When the cold reaches your neck, your skin starts to glow. And then, as your body warms, you die.

Outside the dogs were barking, inside the room nothing rustled, nothing creaked.

Suddenly she felt Paul's hand reaching for her, pulling her to the window. He shoved the heavy drapes aside and lifted the white lace curtain over her hair. You can't do it, he said, look, that's water in the puddle, not ice, the goose tracks in the mud are soft, it didn't freeze. He looked at her, you know, with that white lace on your head you look just like the lamb, he said.

He took off her coat, then her shoes, then her clothes. Adina didn't resist, she simply thought to herself as he did so that his sleep must be transparent, that it's a long, empty corridor where nothing can stay hidden from him, not even what someone nearby is thinking in the dark.

And then there was no anchor, no hold, when he reached for her breasts and past years came back inside her body, the years with Paul. His penis was hot and stubborn, and her skin glowed differently than the desire to freeze to death among the corn. But she knew it wasn't really herself who was glowing. It was their situation. And now the fox was there in the house with them, and Liviu and the lamb were no match for the fox.

Adina sat in the dark next to Paul, his cigarette glowed, he stroked her forehead. The woman who had moaned was no longer there. Is that reproach I'm sensing, he asked. She couldn't make out the wardrobe, but she could see the apricots hovering in their jars below the ceiling. Yes, she said, but that doesn't matter. In fact she didn't see the apricots in their jars, she only knew that they were there.

Because lurking behind everything she did, every movement

of her hand, every step she took, even during her sleep, was the knowledge that Liviu and the lamb were living in a little roadside village, that Christmas was waiting for her with a crippled fir tree, that they would decorate the tree and drag it next to the window for the passersby outside, just like years ago. And that there would be no passersby, at most two strangers who had spent the entire morning crossing the field—a woman with a child who wanted a fox.

As far as you're concerned, said Paul, being separated means I'm always on call for you, but never sleep with you. The cigarette glowed and quickly consumed itself.

Be quiet, said Adina, my head is about to explode.

During the night she dreamed that Clara was standing in the frozen corn wearing a dress with yellow bouquets of roses. The wind had a dry rustle, and Clara was carrying a large bag. She said, there's no one here, they aren't looking for you. She opened the bag. It was full of quinces. Clara said, here, have one, I washed them for you. Adina took a quince and said, no you didn't, there's a bit of fur on the peel.

A black and white sky

Every morning Adina sprinkles a few dried linden blossoms into the boiling water and they swell up as the stems and skin-like bracts turn bright green. To separate one day from the next she keeps count of the times she makes tea. The routine is always the same, it's always morning, and the geese and dogs are always outside on the streets. There's always a note on the table: WE'LL BE BACK AT 12 or 1 or AROUND EVENING. The linden blossom tea always tastes like sleep. The chamber pot stinks next to the kitchen door.

Adina seldom peeks through the gap in the kitchen curtain, because the fences in the yard are made of wire, and the lilac bushes are bare. People can see through the yards and gardens.

But Paul looks out often and reports the color of the sky and the mud and whether it seems cold outside or not.

Earlier in the morning they heard voices coming from the village, and Paul has been sitting at the curtain gap ever since he got up. Here the street is empty, but down in the middle of the village people are hooting and howling.

Adina peers through the gap. The sun is glaring, the bare lilac lays its shadow across the sand. The next-door neighbor is setting up three chairs in her yard. Her face is small and wrinkled. In the sun she has a mustache and no eyes. She carries two pillows and two down covers into the yard and shakes them out and drapes them over the chairs.

Paul's tea has gotten cold, because he's fixated on something behind the curtain roses.

Liviu comes running past the gap, without a coat, his jacket flapping open. Here comes Liviu and he's in a hurry, says Paul, quickly sitting down at the table, where he sips his cold tea. Through the curtain Adina sees Liviu racing past the bare lilac without closing the gate. He's carrying his scarf in his hand. Adina pulls the curtain shut, quickly sits down beside Paul and cradles her head in her hands. The key turns in the door. Liviu's face is red and sweaty, he tosses his scarf on the kitchen table. Can't you hear what's going on outside, he pants, come into the living room.

His hands are shaking, he turns on the TV, they didn't let Ceaușescu speak, he says, the people shouted him down, a bodyguard pulled him back behind the stage. Adina starts to cry, the screen is a blur of stone cubes and windows, a mass of coats surging in front of the Central Committee building, thousands of coats blurred together like a field, with lots of screaming and shouting. Adina's cheeks flush hot, her chin dissolves, her hands are wet, the little screaming faces form a streak of eyes looking skyward. He's running away, Liviu shouts, he's fleeing. He's dead, Paul shouts, if he runs he's dead.

A helicopter hovers above the balcony of the Central

Committee. And then it gets smaller and smaller, a floating gray point of a needle that eventually disappears.

On the screen is an empty black and white sky.

Liviu kisses the screen, I'm going to eat you, I'm going to devour you, he says. His wet kisses linger in the black and white sky. Adina sees the old man's legs, the two angular knees, the white calves, and the forelock high in the sky, higher than ever. Paul opens all the curtains. It's so bright inside that the walls suddenly seem too big for the room, they are shaking with the light.

The lamb is standing in the doorway, still panting from running. She laughs two round tears into her eyes and says, over in front of the church they've stripped the policeman down to his underwear and they're giving him a beating. The accountant pulled off the policeman's pants and the priest hung his cap on a tree.

The old lady next door knows everything, says the lamb. A couple days ago she told me that we're having too warm a winter this year.

Winter lightning, winter thunder
Winter clouds all burst asunder
In December broken sky
Means the king will surely die.

That's how she put it. I'm old, she said, anyway that's the way it used to be. And this morning she asked me if I'd heard anything in the night. Not shots, she said, it was a thunderstorm, but not here, farther out in the country.

Liviu and Paul drink brandy, the bottle gurgles, the glasses clink. Paul marches barefoot around the kitchen table wearing Liviu's robe, glass in hand, singing the forbidden song in a trembling voice:

> Awaken, Romanian, wake from thy deadly slumber

Liviu drapes a crumpled dish towel over his shoulders and dances with the bottle and sings in a high-pitched, whiny voice:

> Merry tomorrow, merry today
> Things move forward day by day

The pots rattle in the kitchen cupboard, Paul leaves the awakening Romanians right in the middle of his song, dances around Liviu and joins in:

> Forward, forward, fuck fuck fuck
> Forward, forward, fuck fuck fuck
> Always forward never stuck

The lamb leans on the stove, so that the neighbor's pillows and down covers are draped behind her shoulder. In the sunlight they seem to be sleeping on the chairs.

Where is the helicopter going to land, asks the lamb, and Paul says, in heaven, in the mud with the little Romanians.

When I was little there used to be a swing carousel next to the market, says the lamb. They'd take it down at the first sign of snow, because Mihai the ticket taker had a stiff leg and couldn't sit out in the cold. If you wanted to ride on the carousel you had to buy tickets at the People's Council office. One ride cost three tickets for children and five for adults. The money was supposed to pay for paving our road with asphalt. Mihai took the tickets and tore a corner off each one and tossed the corners into a hat. In the summer he let the older girls ride for free because before the ride he could stand behind a big packing crate and reach into their pants. A few complained to the mayor, but the mayor said it didn't matter, since it didn't really hurt. Mihai would start up the motor and turn it off to end the ride. All rides lasted the same amount of time, because he kept his eye on the church clock. At noon he took a break, ate lunch and poured a can of diesel oil into the motor. He only repaired the motor at night so as not to lose any business during the day. He knew the motor well since he'd built it himself out of old tractor parts. Occasionally I'd ride too, but only if there were just girls nearby, says the lamb, because when the boys were there they'd grab the seats when the girls were in midair and twist the chains until the girls threw up. They learned that from Mihai.

One winter evening two black cars arrived in the village. They were coming from an inspection at the border. People said there were three high party functionaries, a border officer and three bodyguards. They were all completely plastered. One of them knocked on the mailman's window and asked who had the key to the swing ride. The mailman pointed to the other end of the village, where Mihai lived.

Mihai was already asleep when they knocked on the window. He didn't want to get up, but they insisted. Yes, said Mihai, I have the key, only there isn't any oil in the motor, and I don't have any here, it's over at the People's Council office. But he ended up getting the key anyway and went off with the bodyguard. After looking into the motor he said there was enough oil for one ride. And what happens then, asked the bodyguard. Then the motor will stop, said Mihai.

The bodyguard waved to the others, and they all climbed out of the cars and took their places in the seats, the bodyguards between the functionaries, the border officer last. Mihai waited beside the motor until they'd buckled themselves in. Start it up, said the bodyguard, once it gets going you can go home.

The motor ran, the seats flew, the chains angled out into the air. Mihai went home, the moon shone and it was very cold. But the motor hummed, and the seats flew all night long.

The next morning the carousel was still there, says the lamb, and the seats were hanging in the air, and the seven men were hanging strapped in the seats, frozen to death.

The lamb wipes two tears from her eyes, her mouth opens and closes. The next day a commission came to the village. The carousel was no longer allowed, it was torn down and taken away. The road was never paved. Mihai and the mailman were arrested as class enemies. At the trial Mihai said it was night and the diesel oil was black. He must have made a mistake, the motor was probably full. And the mailman testified that he'd heard the motor running all night long, it didn't get quiet until it was almost morning. Once he'd even looked out the window and seen the comrades flying through the air. Yes, he'd heard their howling, he said, but he hadn't given it a second thought, they looked like they were having a good time.

Frozen raspberries

The black and white sky stayed empty, the forbidden song spread throughout the country in trains, in buses, on horse-drawn carts. In tattered coat pockets and shoes worn down to the point of listing. Also in the car, between Adina and Paul as they drive back to the city.

The sky in the roadside village is blue, the forbidden song has howled it empty. The village policeman put his pants back on but left his cap on the tree. He didn't clear out his desk, just grabbed the pictures of his wife and two children and stashed them in his jacket. Then he cut across the field at the end of the village, looking to get as far away as possible.

The old lady next door carries her pillows and down covers into the house, because evening is lurking behind the village as it does every day, only louder.

At the border, at the other end of the country, where the plain juts into Hungary like the tip of a nose, there is a little crossing. The barrier is dark. A car is waiting by the barrier, the driver is wearing a thick sweater. He hands his passport through the window. The border officer reads:

KARÁCSONYI ALBERT
Mother MAGDA née FURÁK
Father KARÁCSONYI ALBERT

As the man returns his passport to the glove compartment a birthmark the size of a fingertip pops out of his shirt collar. The barrier swings up.

Adina and Paul look up at the window, the curtains have been drawn. The apartment is unlocked, the key has been left in the door from the inside. Abi is not at home and there is no note. The wardrobe is open, a matchbox is lying on the carpet. A chair has been knocked over on the kitchen floor. On the kitchen table is a half-empty bottle of brandy and a full glass. The soup in the pot on the stove has a layer of mold.

No one leaves home like that, says Paul, unless they're forced to.

At the café behind the quiet streets of power the glass panes have been shattered by bullets. The red curtains have been torn down. Soldiers sit at the tables. The poplars rise pointed and tall and peer into the water. Where fishermen stood during the striped summer, soldiers now stand day and night. They don't care what time it is, the bell tolls in the cathedral tower and doesn't even hear itself.

The dark green yews between the opera and the cathedral have been torn apart, the display windows splintered and empty.

The bullet holes on the walls are as dense as skipping black rocks.

The cathedral steps are crammed with thin yellow candles. They flicker at a slant, like the wind. The long red carnations and short white cyclamens have been trampled but are not yet wilted. The steps are guarded by tanks and soldiers. The dwarf is wearing a black armband and sitting on the curb next to a wooden cross. He stretches out his legs so that his brick shoes face the sidewalk. He is selling yellow candles. Attached to the cross is a photograph of a dead man, a young face with a pimple. The mouth smiles and smiles. Adina closes her eyes and an angel with a bullet wound smiles from out of the picture. Paul moves his face close to the photograph. At his feet a woman is sitting behind a cloth spread with candles. She is all muffled up and eating a soft-boiled egg. She bores her fingertip into the yolk and licks it. Her finger and the corner of her mouth and the yolk are yellow just like the candles. The woman wipes her finger on her coat and holds two candles out to Adina and Paul.

Praying is something I just can't do, says Adina, Paul lights one of the candles.

At the opera, a whole gallery of photographs has been posted on the heavy wooden doors. Paul reaches over an old man in a fur cap and points at one of them. His finger touches the picture, it's a photograph of Pavel, mouth smiling, his birthmark just above his shirt collar. Farther down, Adina's finger touches a different face, it's the man who pissed in the river and right afterward was able to walk along the bank like a quiet man. Underneath the pictures are the words: THESE ARE THE ONES WHO FIRED.

They all fired into the air, no doubt about it, said the old man with the fur cap, but it was the air that happened to be in people's lungs.

The curtains have been drawn. They were here all right, says Paul. The door to his apartment is closed. But the doors to the wardrobe are open, the clothes strewn on the floor, the books, the bedspread, the pillow, the blanket. His records are lying on the kitchen tiles, trampled to pieces.

They come to Adina's apartment, she unlocks the front door. The bathroom door is ajar, the sink is empty, no sunflower seed is floating in the toilet. The wardrobe is closed.

The fox tail slides away under the tip of Adina's shoe. Then the first, second and third paw.

And then the fourth.

Adina slides the tail back to the fur with her fingers. Then the right hind paw, then the left, the right forepaw, and the left. That's the right order, she says. Paul inspects the floor. No hair.

Can I stay here, asks Paul.

Adina stands in front of the bathtub, hot water runs out of the pipe, steam coats the mirror. She takes off her blouse, checks the temperature with her hand. Then she turns off the faucet and puts her blouse back on. The TV is talking in the other room.

I looked in the mirror and saw my white shoulders, I saw the bathtub, the white steam, I can't bring myself to get undressed, she says, I can't manage to take a bath. She rummages through her travel bag. The nail clipper is on the bottom.

Before the sheets are warm, sleep has filled their heads. Because both Adina and Paul have gone to bed with the same bullet-pierced image that swells until it bursts through the skull because the image is bigger than their heads.

I loved you like my own children, the dictator's wife had spoken right into the room. The dictator nodded, his eyes saw the nail clipper on the table next to Adina's hand and he pulled his black fur cap down onto his forehead. He'd been wearing the same cap for several days. After that bullets shot through the screen and hit the wall of a barrack, in the filthiest bare corner of the courtyard.

The wall stayed there, empty and riddled with bullet holes.

And then two old peasants were lying on the ground, and the soles of their shoes peered into the room, while heavy soldiers' boots stood in a circle around their heads. Her silk scarf had slid off her head onto her neck. His black fur cap had not. Which one was it, the same, the last.

How about them, would you cut their corpses open, asked Adina. Paul squeezed and released the nail clipper. That would be worse than having to look inside my mother and father, he said. My father often beat me, I was afraid of him. When I saw the way he held his bread while he ate my fear went away. In those moments he and I were the same, we were equal. But when he beat me, I couldn't believe he used the same hand to eat his bread.

Paul was breathing deeply after all the exhaustion of the past days. Where other people have a heart, those two have a cemetery, said Adina, and between their temples there's nothing but dead people, small and bloody like frozen raspberries. Paul rubbed some tears out of his eyes, I am repulsed by them and still I have to cry for them. Where does it come from, he asked, this sympathy.

Two heads on the same pillow, separated by sleep, ears under hair. And above their sleep, behind the city, a lighter but sad day is waiting. Winter and warm air, and the dead are cold. In Abi's kitchen the full glass remains untouched.

A few streets farther on, Clara falls asleep with the same bullet-riddled image. The telephone rings through her sleep. The red-swollen carnations are standing in the dark, the water in the vase casts a gleam. I'm in Vienna, says Pavel, someone is going to drop by soon and give you my address and a passport, you have to come right away, otherwise I won't be here anymore.

I don't know you

The glowing windows sway back and forth as the streetcar rolls ahead on the tracks. Here and there lights appear in the dark streets. Anyone who is awake behind the walls has light in their windows. Anyone who's awake at this hour has to go to the factory. The hand grips dangle from their rails, the dwarf is sitting next to the door. The tracks squeal. A woman with a child on her arm is seated next to Clara. The door bangs at every stop, and the child sighs, and the dwarf closes his eyes, and the door opens. And no one comes in, just sand blown inside by the wind. The sand is like flour, only dark. It can't be seen, it can only be heard scratching on the floor.

The streetcar reaches the corner where the fence is right next to the tracks. A branch grazes the brightly lit window, and the child sings with an absent voice:

The worries refuse to leave me alone
Must I sell my field and my house and my home

The child's mother lowers her head and looks at the empty floor, the dwarf lowers his head, Clara lowers her head. The rails sing along below their shoes. The grip handles listen as they swing.

The loudspeaker at the factory gate is mute, the striped cat is sitting beside the entrance. The slogans have moved from the halls into the courtyard. The dwarf walks into the yard, his brick shoes clatter. The striped cat goes padding behind him.

Grigore is now the director, the director is the foreman, the gateman is the warehouse supervisor, the foreman is the gateman.

Crizu is dead.

And an hour later, when it's brighter outside and the housing blocks are huddled together under the gray sky, Adina passes through the same morning on her way to school. Inside the broken phone booth is a crust of bread. At the end of the street is the large spool of wire. In the yard outside the wooden shack is an empty chain. Olga the dog is no longer there.

In the filthiest bare corner of the school yard, in front of a wall, is a mountain. Half of the mountain is cloth, woven cords, yellow tassels, epaulettes. The other half is paper, slogans, provincial emblems, brochures and newspapers with speeches and pictures.

The child with eyes set far apart and narrow temples is carrying a picture in front of him. The picture shows the forelock and the black inside the eye. The picture is on its side, the forelock reaches down to the child's shoes. We're not burning the frame, says the servant's daughter. She tears the forelock out of the frame, my mother's in the officer's house all by herself, she says, the officer has been arrested, and his wife is in hiding. The twins bring a basket with youth pioneer kerchiefs and red pioneer flags with yellow fringes.

The servant's daughter holds a match to the half of the mountain made of paper. The fire quickly eats its way higher and higher, the hard paper curls like gray ears. Do you know how long I've been waiting for this, says the servant's daughter. The soft paper disintegrates, I'd never have guessed, says Adina. The twins skewer burning silk fringe onto a couple sticks and go running through the school yard. What was I supposed to do, says the servant's daughter, I had to keep quiet, I have a child. The wind blows the smoke over the wall. The child with eyes set far apart stands next to Adina and listens.

I know, says Adina, the men had wives, the wives had children, the children were hungry. The servant's daughter pulls a strand of hair through her mouth, looks at the half-burned mountain, anyway now it's over, she says, and we're alive. Next week I'll come visit you.

The servant's daughter is the director of the school, the director is the coach, the coach is the union leader, the physicist is in charge of transition and democracy.

The cleaning woman wanders through the halls with a broom and dusts the empty walls where the pictures used to hang.

Adina leans against the gate, the smoke is still rising from the school yard. There are pictures posted downtown, says Adina, your good person was one of the ones who fired. And you had a birthday. Even if I'd been here, I wouldn't have been able to give you anything, no shoes, no dress, no blouse. Not even an apple. If you can't give someone something then that person is a stranger.

He didn't fire at anyone, says Clara, he's out of the country. Her eyelids have a blue shimmer, I have a passport, she says, what should I do. Her eyelashes are long and thick and calm.

I don't know you, says Adina, you have no business here.

From the sixth floor Adina and the servant's daughter watch as a warm winter afternoon passes behind the stadium. On the table is a bottle of brandy and two glasses. Adina and the servant's daughter clink and drain their glasses. A single drop trickles back to the bottom of each glass.

The servant's daughter has brought her daughter who is two and a half years old. The girl sits on the rug and rubs her cheek with the tail of the fox. She talks to herself. Adina refills the glasses. The neighbor with the chestnut-red hair done up in big waves is standing by her open window.

Look, this cat has a mustache, says the child. Under her fingertips the fox's head slides away from the neck. The child lays the fox head on the table.

For the second time, Adina feels a noise in her head like a branch breaking. Only different.

The servant's daughter raises her glass.

That doesn't matter, doesn't matter at all

Past the last bridge there are no flagstones along the riverbank, no benches, no poplars, no soldiers.

At the bottom of the box are the fox's paws, on top of them the body, and the tail. On the very top is the head. Clara gave me this box, says Adina. We were coming from town, she bought a pair of shoes and put them on right away.

Paul closes the box.

You know, I had planned on keeping that fox, says Adina. Sitting at the table or standing at the wardrobe or lying in bed, I wasn't afraid of it anymore. Paul sticks his finger through the middle of the lid, for the candle, he says, and sets the candle inside the hole. And now they've cut off the head as well, she says, but the fox is still the hunter. The candle burns, Paul sets the box on the water.

He lets it go.

Then he looks up at the sky, Abi is up there, he says, looking down on us. That doesn't matter, doesn't matter at all, he says, crying. The burning candle looks like a finger. Maybe Ilie really does know what he's doing, he says.

Night spreads, the shoe box floats.

And far off in the country, near where the plain comes to an end, where everyone knows every little path, a place so far away that it's barely reached by the same night, Ilie is cutting across a field. He is wearing his soldier's uniform and his clunky boots and he's carrying a small suitcase. The train station is off by itself, and where the sky stops, the lights of the small town are glowing, one next to another like the stripes on a border barrier. Now the border isn't so far away.

Inside the waiting room there are no wall newspapers, the cabinets are empty except for the dust left from summer. The station attendant is eating sunflower seeds.

Timişoara, says Ilie.

The attendant spits some seeds through the window at the counter. Round-trip, he asks.

Just one way, says Ilie. His heart is pounding.

The earthen wall of the stadium pulls the bare brush closer. The last goal has been forgotten, the forbidden song has sung itself throughout the country, and now, as it spreads, it presses against the throat and turns mute. Because the tanks are still scattered throughout the town, and the bread line in front of the store is still long. Above the earthen wall the long-distance runner dangles his naked legs over the city, and one coat slinks into another.

ABOUT THE TRANSLATOR

PHILIP BOEHM has won numerous awards for his translations from German and Polish, including works by Franz Kafka, Christoph Hein, Hanna Krall, and Stefan Chwin. He also works as a theater director and playwright: produced plays include *Mixtitlan*, *The Death of Atahualpa*, and *Return of the Bedbug*. He lives in St. Louis, where he is the artistic director of Upstream Theater.

Also by Herta Müller and available from Granta Books
www.grantabooks.com

THE LAND OF GREEN PLUMS

Herta Müller

Translated by Michael Hofmann

WINNER OF THE INTERNATIONAL IMPAC DUBLIN LITERARY AWARD

'This is a genuinely moving book. The style . . . develops an almost hypnotic power over the reader' *Sunday Telegraph*

Set in Romania at the height of Ceauşescu's reign of terror, *The Land of Green Plums* tells the story of a group of young students, each of whom has left the impoverished provinces in search of better prospects in the city. It is a profound illustration of a totalitarian state which comes to inhabit every aspect of life; to the extent that everyone, even the strongest, must either bend to the oppressors, or resist them and perish.

'A powerful autobiographical account, *The Land of Green Plums* . . . will linger on in the mind and Michael Hofmann's translation is a marvel' *Guardian*

'*The Land of Green Plums* is a miracle, a fearless human testimony which operates through the combined force of Müller's tight, understated eloquence and Hofmann's deft, atmospheric translation' *Irish Times*

'If W. G. Sebald's *The Emigrants* suggested there are still new ways of writing about exile and the Holocaust, *The Land of Green Plums* promises similar possibilities for the literature of the Iron Curtain' *Literary Review*

Also by Herta Müller and available from Portobello Books
www.portobellobooks.com

THE HUNGER ANGEL

Herta Müller

Translated by Philip Boehm

'Müller takes us beyond pain, beyond politics and into the unrecognisable . . . her extraordinarily clear and dispassionate novel is testament to one man's survival' *Independent*

The end of WWII is fast approaching when 17-year-old Leo Auberg is deported from his small Romanian town to a Soviet labour camp. He carries with him his father's overcoat, a suitcase fashioned from a gramophone box, his aunt's green woollen gloves, a copy of *Faust*, and these words from his grandmother: 'I know you'll come back.'

From the 2009 Nobel Laureate comes a masterpiece that sings of suffering and endurance, taking us beyond one man's physical toil into the depths of the human soul.

'This is not just a good novel, it is a great one; a work of literature that deserves a place on the shelf beside *One Day in the Life of Ivan Denisovich* . . . There are many sentences of this masterpiece you will want to copy out or commit to memory' A. N. Wilson, *Financial Times*

'A book which can exert a spell' *Scotsman*

'A remarkable novel, both bleak and chastening' Helen Dunmore, *Guardian*

Also by Herta Müller and available from Portobello Books
www.portobellobooks.com

CRISTINA AND HER DOUBLE

Herta Müller

Translated by Geoffrey Mulligan

A selection of essays that confirms Herta Müller's status as one of the most fearless and incandescent European literary figures of the last fifty years.

Does living in a dictatorship change the way you see things?

Is there beauty to be found in an empty can of Coca-Cola in the apartment of a hungry citizen?

How can a simple colloquialism unlock the secrets of the movement of the wind, or the resting of the swallows?

Exactly what information is held in the files of Romania's Securitate?

... and hypnotic, Herta Müller's extraordinary essays
... held Communist Romania
... complicity,

Also by Herta Müller and available from Portobello Books
www.portobellobooks.com

THE APPOINTMENT

Herta Müller

Translated by Michael Hulse and Philip Boehm

'A brooding, fog-shrouded allegory of life under the long oppression of the regime of Nicolae Ceauşescu' *New York Times*

A young seamstress in a clothing factory has been summoned for questioning. This is not the first time she has been called in, but this time she knows it will be worse. As she rides the tram to her interrogation, her thoughts stray to her friends and family, many of them killed or destroyed by the brutal government. In her distraction, she misses her stop and there, on an unfamiliar street, she discovers something that suddenly puts her fear of the appointment into chilling perspective.

'Nobody since Arthur Koestler in the 1940s has written more intelligently or with such subtle precision about life under totalitarianism . . . Müller has an exceptionally rare talent – to turn the terrifying, the distorted and the hideously ugly into something uplifting and beautiful' *Pr*...onal, yet ...attention' *Herald*

'*Th*...

'A slim, masterfully written tale' *Newsweek*